RACHEL AND HERMAN

MINA LEWITON

AND

RACHEL
HERMAN

PICTURES BY HOWARD SIMON

FRANKLIN WATTS, Inc.

New York

1957

For the descendants of the pioneers
who took the northward route: from
Downtown to Uptown.

"Rachel, Rachel, wake up," Momma called. "Did you forget what day this is?"

In her sleep Rachel remembered what day it was. She opened her eyes and looked through the door to the kitchen.

A great brown and white dog stared back at her from the upper half of the calendar on the kitchen wall. A little barrel on a chain hung around the dog's white fur neck. Underneath was the September calendar. She could easily read its large numbers.

Poppa had put a red crayon circle around the 9 to show it was the first day of school. Today was the ninth.

Rachel looked away from the calendar and thought of her old school Downtown. All her friends would be there today. If she opened the door of the 6A1 classroom of P.S. 31 this morning, everyone would know her and she would know everyone. But she wasn't going to P.S. 31 this morning. She was going to the new school Uptown, P.S. 27. Not one single person in the class would know her.

Rachel dressed slowly. Last of all she put on her starched blue and white striped dress that had a sailor collar and a blue tie.

She thought about Miss Beck, who had been her teacher Downtown, and wondered if she would ever see her again. Maybe Miss Beck wouldn't recognize her. First she wouldn't. Then she would.

"Rachel? Oh yes, Rachel Lessing," Miss Beck would say. "Of course I recognize you, but you are much taller now. Would you be the Monitor, Rachel, while I go out of the room?" Miss Beck would be exactly the same.

"Good-by," said Momma to Rachel and to Herman, as they were leaving. "Here in the brown bag is your lunch, Rachel. The white one is Herman's. Poppa and I are going Downtown this morning. We'll be back before you come home. Be a good boy, Herman."

"Good-by," said Rachel, wishing she were going Downtown too, to her old friends and her old school and Miss Beck and the Library and the house they used to live in.

Though it was the first day of school and the ninth of September, it was as warm as a day in summer. Rachel and Herman took a short cut through St. Mary's Park instead of walking around it.

Herman stopped for a drink at the fountain. Then he walked on a little way and went back for another drink. Rachel walked back with him. They saw two squirrels hurry around a tree. Rachel and Herman stood watching the squir-

3

rels scurry up, then down, then around the tree.

"I want another drink," said Herman, and went back.

"Come on," said Rachel. "You'll get your shirt wet."

"No, I won't." Herman put his finger on the spout and aimed a stream of water at the squirrels at the foot of the tree. The stream of water didn't quite reach them, but the squirrels ran up the tree

4

trunk. Herman tried for the high branches with the water.

"Stop," said Rachel. "You'll get wet. You'll get both of us wet."

Herman's shirt and especially his collar were starched. He moved his neck stiffly as he shook his head.

"No, I won't," he said. His finger slipped and a stream of water accidentally came his way.

The squirrels scrambled down the tree.

"It only got a little wet," he said, while Rachel tried to dry off his shirt with her folded handkerchief.

"Why did they go Downtown?" asked Herman, as they walked away from the fountain.

"I don't know," Rachel said, but she thought it was because their new bookstore was becoming more and more of a worry to Poppa.

"Uptown is a very quiet place," Poppa had said yesterday. "There are few customers for books. So far. Perhaps it was a mistake to move Uptown."

"We must wait a little while longer," Momma had answered, "before we talk about mistakes."

But if there were so few customers and it had

been a mistake to move Uptown, they could move Downtown again where there were more people who bought books. She would go back to her old school then, and have all her old friends again. She was thinking of what to say when she saw Miss Beck again. "I've come back," she'd say, and Miss Beck would say, "I certainly missed you, Rachel. Would you take the Attendance?"

"Look," said Herman, stopping suddenly and pointing.

Rachel looked.

From the top of the high iron picket fence built around the park a young, thin, gray cat was watching the squirrels too. The cat walked along the fence, stopping every now and then, one paw raised, to stare round-eyed at the squirrels, now joined by a third squirrel and still chasing each other.

Suddenly the cat leaped from the fence to the tree trunk and climbed after the squirrels, which disappeared up the tree.

"Come on," said Rachel. "It's getting late."

"Wait," said Herman. "Let's see if the cat can get down."

6

"Come on," said Rachel.

"Wait," said Herman.

Rachel saw that the cat had scrambled up and then had turned around to come down. His two front feet were braced against the tree trunk. The cat was looking about helplessly as if he really couldn't get down.

Meow. The little cat's voice was surprisingly loud. *Meow.*

"I'll get him down," Herman said. "Hold this, Rachel." He slipped out of his jacket and handed it and his lunch to her, and his ruler and pencil box.

"It's your new shirt, Herman," Rachel said, holding his arm.

7

"I'll be careful," Herman said, pulling free.

Herman climbed up a little way and reached for the cat, but the cat leaped farther up the tree —then came down an inch or two, looked helplessly about once more, and meowed.

Herman climbed up a little higher. He tried to catch the cat with one hand, but slipped down the tree trunk a little way. Rachel heard the sound of tearing.

"I almost got him," said Herman. He began climbing up again. He reached a sturdy branch and held on. The cat was hidden in thick leaves.

"Come down, Herman," Rachel called. "I see someone running to school. It must be late. It's the first day, Herman. We'll be late the first day."

Herman made a sweeping lunge and caught the cat by the tail. The cat yowled as if he were dying. Down came Herman, sliding most of the way with the yowling cat under one arm. At the foot of the tree the cat turned a somersault out of Herman's hands and, like a shot, was off.

Rachel stared at Herman. Two ribbons of shirt hung down in front. Both Herman's arms were scratched. The part of the shirt that wasn't torn had brown bark stains all over it.

Herman looked down at himself too. "I'll wash my hands," he said.

He went to the fountain and sent up a spout of water and washed first one hand and then the

other and even his face. Rachel unfolded her damp handkerchief and helped him dry off.

Herman put on his jacket. "Maybe he'd have never come down," Herman said. "Maybe he'd have stayed there the whole day and the whole night until somebody got him down. Maybe a policeman would have to get him down."

"Let's hurry," Rachel said. She picked up the lunches that she had laid down while drying off Herman. The sun had warmed the lunch bags and something inside one of them had begun to melt, either the cheese or the butter. Rachel and

Herman ran all the rest of the way to school.

The school halls had the lonely and frightening air of lateness.

"Come with me, Rachel," said Herman. "I'm scared to go to my room by myself."

Rachel took him to Room 114. They looked inside. Two people, one of them the teacher, were at the back of the room, talking.

Rachel buttoned up Herman's coat over the torn shirt. Herman slipped into an empty seat. Then she hurried up a stairway and down a hall and found Room 304.

Miss Bannerman was the teacher. She stood at the front of the room, a sheet of paper pinned to form a cuff over each sleeve. Her white waist had ruffles in a row marching down the front of it. Miss Bannerman's black skirt was pleated and long. Her hair was swept up high from her forehead. Rachel saw at once that Miss Bannerman was nothing like Miss Beck, who smelled like flowers and talked softly and smiled.

"It is too bad," said Miss Bannerman to the class, brushing off chalk dust from her hands, "that we cannot have Perfect Attendance on the first day of school. And on a fine, bright, sunny morning like this."

At the blackboard Miss Bannerman had written,

Present   31
Absent   1
Late   0

Everyone looked out of the window. Feathery heaps of white clouds floated lazily in the bright blue sky.

"May I have your attention," Miss Bannerman said, "or would you rather stare out of the window?" Miss Bannerman did not expect anyone to answer this. No one did.

Then she saw Rachel. "Better late than never," Miss Bannerman remarked. She picked up the chalk and shifted the 0 and 1 beside the words *Late* and *Absent*.

"Are you Rachel Lessing?"

Rachel nodded.

"Raise your hand, Gladys Mahoney. Rachel, go and sit in front of Gladys."

Gladys kept her hand up like a thin guidepost,

and Rachel tiptoed across the room. She slipped
into the seat in front of Gladys.

A big boy at the back of the room raised his
hand.

"Don't waste our time, George, unless you have
an important question. Is it an important question?"

George nodded as if he were trying to shake his
head off.

"What is it, George?"

"You didn't change the 31 to 32."

"Thank you, George. I am glad one person is

alert," said Miss Bannerman, erasing and changing the 31 to 32. "I am going to be very strict this term." Miss Bannerman looked around at the class severely, as if they had already done something wrong.

Everyone looked unhappy.

"Very, very strict." Then Miss Bannerman said, "Rachel, fill out this Late Slip. When the bell rings for noontime dismissal, take it to the Principal's Office."

Rachel went to get the Late Slip, and returned to her seat. The Late Slip said,

> Name ....
> Class ....
> Reason for Lateness .....
>
> ....

She filled in her name and wrote 6A1 beside Class and thought about what she could write next to Reason for Lateness. There wasn't enough room to write all that had happened to make her late this morning, but the main reason was the cat. She therefore wrote CAT. Then she put the Late Slip into the pocket of her blue and white striped dress.

2

"Boys on this side for a spelling match," Miss Bannerman was saying. "Girls on the side near the window."

Rachel moved quickly into the girls' line. If there was anything she loved, it was a spelling match.

"George, you can be the Window Monitor. Open the windows wide, please, for Deep Breathing. *In,* one. *Out,* two. One . . . two . . . one . . . two . . ."

Everyone breathed in and out deeply and noisily.

"Stop. Now put on your thinking caps," ordered Miss Bannerman.

Everyone stopped breathing in and out noisily and resumed normal breathing. A big boy who wore eyeglasses clapped his hand on top of his head to show he was putting on his thinking cap. Miss Bannerman looked sternly at him.

While waiting for her own word, Rachel looked at the girls and boys in her new class and spelled their words to herself.

In a way it was like Miss Beck's class last term. Some of these girls and boys were short and fat and some were tall and thin. One girl looked a little like Becky Eisen and another one looked like Fanny Essig. But their names weren't like the Downtown names. They were like names in books: Tom Donahue and John Davis and Gladys Mahoney. Tom had round blue eyes and he was rubbing them as if just awakened from sleep. Lizzie Stein had dark red hair and pink cheeks. She was wearing a green gingham dress and a green band in her hair. Lizzie in the green gingham was beautiful and so was Gladys, who had light brown hair and blue eyes and wore a pink dress.

"Pigeon," said Miss Bannerman to Rachel, who spelled it right.

"Watch out," Miss Bannerman warned the class, "we have a good speller here."

It was going to be hard to love Miss Bannerman as she had loved Miss Beck of 5B1 Downtown, but it seemed to Rachel that Miss Bannerman was improving a little.

"Moreover," said Miss Bannerman. Almost all the rest of the class missed that one. "Moreover," said Miss Bannerman to Lizzie Stein, who spelled it right.

The words came faster and faster. Recipe for Rachel. Dictionary for Lizzie. Likable for John Davis, who spelled it wrong.

There were only three people left. Tom Donahue and Lizzie Stein and Rachel.

"Now," said Miss Bannerman, "one easy word for each girl and then we'll get on to the hard ones. Only," said Miss Bannerman to Rachel.

Only. Was it only or olny? Only one, Rachel

said to herself, seeing it plainly written out in the air. It sounded right and looked right, but so did—

"That's the easy one, Rachel Lessing. Come on." Miss Bannerman snapped her fingers.

Everyone in the class began to raise hands and wave them in the air.

"O-L-N-Y," Rachel spelled.

"Wrong," said Miss Bannerman. "Sit down, Rachel."

Lizzie Stein spelled it right and was the one who won the spelling match.

It was a hundred times worse to miss an easy word like ONLY than a hard one.

Then an even worse thing happened.

The door opened and a boy walked up to Miss Bannerman's desk. In his hand was a brown paper bag. He held it as if he'd just blown it up, the bulging part under his closed hand with the top of the bag spread out and ruffled.

"Anyone leave this lunch down in 114?" the boy asked Miss Bannerman.

"Hold it up," said Miss Bannerman, writing at her desk. "Hold it up for the class to see."

18

The boy held up the brown paper bag. In the middle of it there was a round grease spot. It seemed to be growing larger and larger as Rachel looked at it. Everyone giggled. He waved the wrinkled, grease-spotted brown bag slowly in the air and the class began to laugh.

Rachel leaned over the inkwell and examined it carefully to see if there was any ink in it.

"Not in this room," said Miss Bannerman, looking up for a moment.

"That's what she said in the office," said the boy, going toward the door.

"Is *she* the cat's mother?" asked Miss Bannerman, as if she were terribly angry.

"Miss White," said the boy, hurrying toward the door.

"Don't slam the door," shouted Miss Bannerman.

When the door closed, Rachel straightened up.

"Tom Donahue, you can be the Book Monitor," said Miss Bannerman. "Give these out, please."

Mathematics, Sixth Grade. The words were printed in white on the bright blue covers. They were brand-new books, with the pleasant smells of glue and new paper about them. Rachel's Arithmetic crackled when she opened it.

"Rachel Lessing," said Miss Bannerman, "you may give out the arithmetic paper."

Even though she had been late, Miss Bannerman was letting her be the Paper Monitor. Miss Bannerman was getting to be almost as nice as Miss Beck.

Rachel handed each girl and boy a sheet of un-lined paper.

"Do the examples on pages 1 and 2. Be sure to number your answers. I am going to mark for neatness."

In the quiet room everyone did examples and proved answers. The sunshine slanted into the room and George Davis was told to lower the window shades halfway.

The examples were easy. Rachel finished them and looked around the room. Then she looked out of the window. The clouds were gone. The sky remained deepest, brightest blue. She wondered whether the boy had really taken her lunch to the Principal's Office. Perhaps he had thrown it away instead. She was suddenly hungry. She was very sorry she hadn't asked for her lunch quickly, before he began waving it in the air.

Rachel looked at her paper once more and proved all the answers in the first line over again. She chewed the top of her pencil and then proved all the examples on the next line, too.

"Are you hungry, Rachel?" asked Miss Banner-man.

Rachel was surprised. She looked at Miss Bannerman as if Miss Bannerman could read minds, or rather stomachs.

Miss Bannerman didn't expect an answer. "Don't chew your pencil," she said.

Rachel glanced at the top of her pencil. It was ragged from chewing. But it was true. She was terribly hungry.

"If you are through with all the examples and have proved them," Miss Bannerman said to Rachel, "you may take the Attendance Sheet down to the Principal's Office."

It was exactly as if Miss Bannerman were turning into Miss Beck—into an Uptown Miss Beck.

3

Rachel took the Attendance Sheet, went down two flights of stairs, and walked along the hall until she came to the Principal's Office. It was a long, dim room and at the far end of it someone was putting papers on shelves in a closet. Rachel could hear the rustle of the papers and she could also hear the sound of her own breathing.

Then she saw *it*.

There lay her brown lunch bag in an open wooden box on a desk. The paper bag looked even more wrinkled and untidy than when the boy had held it up in Room 304. Inside the bag, she knew, was a sandwich made of pumpernickel bread and two slices of Swiss cheese. Maybe an apple too, and maybe a peppermint. Her stomach hurt with hunger. If she could just reach for it, she could stuff the bag into the square pocket of her dress. She could keep her hand over it on the way upstairs and then quickly put it into her desk.

Rachel held her breath. Then she reached over and snatched the brown paper bag, and in an instant it was in her pocket. As she pushed it down into her pocket, her fingers touched the Late Slip. Instead of her lunch, she put the Late Slip into the open wooden box.

Her heart thumped against her ribs. She rattled the Attendance Sheet and then said aloud, "This is the Attendance Sheet. From Miss Bannerman. It's for you," while trying to keep her voice from sounding shaky. "It's for you, Miss White," Rachel repeated.

"You'll find a box for Attendance Sheets," said Miss White, not turning around.

Rachel looked about her and saw on a nearby table the box Miss White meant. She put Miss Bannerman's on top of the other Attendance Sheets.

Rachel hurried back, keeping her hand in her pocket over her bulging lunch. She came into the room as everyone was opening another book that had just been given out. One, nearly new, lay on her desk. This time it was a green book. *Stepping Stones to Literature, Book* 6.

It was like meeting an old friend. They had read *Stepping Stones to Literature, Book* 5, in Miss Beck's class.

Rachel looked over the shoulder of the girl in front of her. Her book was open to page 4. Rachel turned to page 4.

Tom Donahue was reading aloud,

> *The snow had begun in the gloaming*
> *And busily all the night*
> *Had been—*

The gong sounded. Tom Donahue stopped reading.

Rachel hurried down to Herman's class. Herman stood waiting at the door, looking up and down the hall.

"Here I am," said Rachel. "I saw a Lunch Room sign on a door downstairs. Come on."

They walked to the Gym. A cardboard sign was tacked on the Gym door:

LUNCH ROOM.

They opened the door and looked in. No one else was there. The Gym had a deserted, rainy-day smell of dampness and left-over rubbers.

"Let's go to the park," Herman said. "Everyone in my class goes to the park. When they bring their lunch, they go to the park. That's what Jimmy said. Maybe we can find the cat. Come on. If we find him, we can bring him back to school until three o'clock. We can put him in the Lunch Room. Then we can take him home."

"No, we can't. Come on, Herman, we'll go out and eat our sandwiches in the park. Do your scratches hurt?"

Herman shrugged his shoulders.

Just as Miss Bannerman said, it was a bright, sunny day. Rachel and Herman went into the park and found a bench and began to eat their sandwiches.

"Do you like your teacher, Herman?"

"Nope." He glanced quickly at his hands and his fingernails.

Rachel looked at Herman's hands too. "You have to stop biting your nails, Herman."

"That's what Miss Flopsom says."

"Who?"

"Miss Flopsom. It's written on my pencil box." Herman took his pencil box out of his pocket.

"Miss Mary Folsom," said Rachel, reading.

Herman shrugged his shoulders and took a bite of apple. A few squirrels came out and had a look at both of them and came a little closer. One jumped up on the bench. Herman held out a corner of his sandwich and the squirrel came up and got it.

"He's a trained squirrel," said Herman, and gave him the rest of his sandwich. "Where's that cat? I wonder where that cat is." He looked around and up in the trees and along the fence and under benches.

They walked around the fountain and down a path that went to the smallest children's swings. It was very warm, but Herman kept his coat on. They saw a white poodle puppy on a leash that a little girl held. The puppy barked a high, thin bark, listening to himself and barking, and stopping and barking again to hear himself bark.

Boys and girls began to walk through the park on their way back to school from lunch.

"If we had a penny we could buy a candy apple," said Herman. "Or ices."

"Maybe tomorrow," Rachel said. "What did you do this morning, Herman?"

"I got all the examples wrong. Rachel, a boy in my class takes drum lessons."

Lizzie Stein hurried up the school steps. She looked at Rachel and then quickly looked away without even smiling. That would never happen Downtown. Nobody was so stuck-up. Maybe everyone was like Lizzie, thought Rachel. Then she would never find a friend. It made her feel lonely.

"You want me to take you to your class, Herman?"

"Nope," said Herman, running ahead.

"Wait for me," Rachel shouted after him. "Three o'clock."

All afternoon Rachel's class drew a flower pot with a red geranium in it. In the middle of the afternoon Gladys Mahoney tapped Rachel's shoulder and offered her a yellow crayon. She showed Rachel another one she had for herself. Gladys really was lovely and not a bit stuck-up.

Miss Bannerman said Rachel's shading was very good, and pinned up her drawing on the wall. Rachel was sorry when Miss Bannerman said it was Clean-up Time.

It had turned into a lovely first day, after all. Except for being late and except for the lunch bag and Herman's torn shirt and Lizzie's hurrying by without smiling, it was a perfect day. This school was almost as nice to go to as P.S. 31. And there was St. Mary's Park across the street. Someday they'd even go to Bronx Park which, Poppa said, was only a short ride on the trolley.

Just before three o'clock someone came in with a note.

"You are wanted in the Principal's Office, Rachel," said Miss Bannerman. Everyone stared at Rachel. It was surely because she had stolen her lunch out of the box, thought Rachel. Miss White must have seen her and reported her. Rachel walked slowly out of the room.

Miss Wiggam, who was the Principal, put on her eyeglasses when Rachel came into her office.

"Rachel Lessing, what is the meaning of this?" She held up Rachel's Late Slip. "What is the meaning of c-a-t as an excuse for lateness?"

Rachel was relieved. It wasn't about the stolen

lunch anyway. Or at least it wasn't yet. She said,
"We were going to school and—"

"Who is—*we*?"

"My brother and me."

"My brother and *I*."

"My brother and *you*. I mean, Herman and I.
We went into the park and there were squirrels,
and a cat was chasing the squirrels and it ran up
a tree after them. A little gray cat. And it couldn't
come down and it was meowing and Herman said

he would get the cat and come right down and then the cat ran higher and higher up into the tree and then he caught his shirt—"

"The cat's shirt?" asked Miss Wiggam, shaking her finger at Rachel.

"Yes, ma'am. No, ma'am. Herman's shirt and the cat scratched him and then he ran away— the cat ran away . . ." Rachel stopped to take a breath.

"I see," said Miss Wiggam, taking her glasses off again and tapping the desk with them. "In the future, you must come straight to school. Cats usually find their way down to the ground by themselves. Is that clear, Rachel?"

"Yes, ma'am," Rachel said, and ran back to her classroom just as Miss Bannerman was saying, "Class dismissed!"

Herman carried three books home.

"You want me to help you with your homework, Herman?"

"It's easy. Jimmy showed me the examples. I like Miss Folsom," said Herman unexpectedly. "She let me sing. By myself."

"What did you sing?"

32

Herman began to sing:

> *By Killarney's lakes and fells*
> *Emer'ld isles and seas of green . . .*

It was a song Poppa sang with feeling, as he did the folk songs he remembered from his child-hood. A steward had sung it on the ship on which

Poppa had come to America. It was Poppa's favorite American song.

When they came to their house, Herman pressed his finger on the bell and held it there.

There was a clicking sound at the lock. Rachel leaned against the door and almost fell inside. Mr. Feeney, the Superintendent, was coming out with a stepladder. Herman helped Mr. Feeney ease it out.

"O.K., Herman. I got it. I have to put up a sign."

"Let's see," said Herman.

Mr. Feeney showed Herman the sign, white letters on shiny dark blue:

NO CATS OR DOGS ALLOWED.

Herman walked quietly upstairs. It was only at the third floor that Herman took out his ruler and held it against the iron spindles of the stair rail as he ran up.

Momma was waiting at the door. She looked very happy. "Rachel, Herman, look, we have a letter."

"Let me see the stamps," said Herman.

"Guess who is coming," said Momma, raising the letter out of Herman's reach.

"Aunt Frayda?" said Rachel. No, it couldn't be. It would never make Momma so happy. Also, Aunt Frayda never wrote a letter. She came.

"A letter from Boris. Cousin Boris is coming to America! He is already on the ship!"

"Cousin Boris?" It was like saying Rumpelstiltskin was coming to visit them, or Prince Charming. No, not Rumpelstiltskin. It was exactly as if Momma had said Prince Charming was coming to visit them.

4

"When Boris will come . . ." From now on almost everything Momma said began that way. Momma would say, "When Boris will come, Herman, he will help you with your homework." Or, "When Boris will come he will sing for us. He knows hundreds, maybe thousands, of songs, Rachel."

"When Boris will come," said Poppa, "there ought to be quince jam. Boris always liked quince jam. It happens that I too like it. I remember one winter evening very well. As usual, it was snowing. Winter begins early in Chernovinsk," Poppa said to Rachel. "And lasts a long time. Until springtime the snow covers the ground and is piled higher than one's head. And what does one do those long, white winter evenings? The whole family sits comfortably in a warm room, drinking tea and exchanging stories. The evening I speak of we all drank tea and Boris, who had returned from far travels, had much to tell us."

"He has been everywhere," said Momma.

"That evening Boris happened to remark that the wolves of Poland are fiercer than the Russian wolves. A neighbor who was visiting us stated flatly that there were no fiercer wolves than the ones outside Chernovinsk. So those two were discussing the whole question of wolves and, while having this discussion, Boris ate a jar of quinces. Not a small jam jar, but one of those old-fashioned tall quart jars filled with homemade jam. Inch by inch, the jam disappeared."

Rachel could see it all, exactly as if she were there, even the snow settled in the corners of the little windowpanes, and the disappearing quince jam.

Momma asked, "How can you remember these trifles?"

"I don't know," said Poppa. "I have a memory for detail, I suppose. Boris," Poppa added, "likes to tell funny stories. Also he likes animals and, what is more, they like him. Our three dogs always seemed to belong to *him,* although they were actually dogs that belonged to all of us and lived in our house. Although they didn't see Boris for months at a time, no sooner was he home than they were immediately inseparable from him."

"What were their names?" asked Herman.

"Hero," said Poppa, "was one, and the second was Wanderer, and the third, Racer."

"No cats?" Herman asked.

"Why no cats? Certainly, cats. Several cats," said Poppa. "There were always several cats about our house, too."

"Can I have a kitten?" said Herman.

"Positively no," said Momma. "There is a sign downstairs that says NO CATS OR DOGS ALLOWED. This is not Chernovinsk. This is Uptown and they do not allow cats. Or dogs." She looked at Poppa.

38

reproachfully for having brought up the subject of their many dogs and cats.

"It doesn't say NO KITTENS," said Herman. "Jimmy Johnson has a cat. And three kittens. He said I could have one."

"Positively no kittens, too," said Momma.

"If I had a kitten," said Herman. "I could train it to sit next to me while I did homework."

"Speaking of animals," said Poppa hastily, "I can tell you a story of Boris's childhood. One day Boris decides to go for a ride on a horse. He was very small. No more than a year old or so."

"Maybe three years old. Or even four," said Momma. "A child of one cannot ride on a horse. Especially alone. A child of one is a baby."

"Perhaps, but it seems to me he was no more

than one year old. However, Boris gets up on the horse and off goes the horse."

"Someone must have lifted him up on the horse," said Momma.

"Perhaps. I don't remember exactly," said Poppa. "It seems to me he even got up on the horse by himself."

"Positively no," said Momma.

"However he managed it," Poppa said, "Boris rides along for a while and it happens that the horse becomes thirsty. Coming to a stream, the horse bends his head and begins to drink. You can imagine what happens. Here is the horse's neck." Poppa inclined his arm, his hand flat on the table. "And here is Boris." Poppa touched the tip of his upright elbow. "Of course, Boris slides down and into the water. But," said Poppa, "instead of crying as any other child would, Boris, finding himself in the stream, begins to swim. Later, when we go out to look for the missing Boris, we are astonished to see the horse by himself, drinking quietly at the stream, and there in the middle of the water is Boris, swimming about like a fish."

Rachel could see this, too, as if it were a photograph, only now the scene was changed to a lovely summer day.

"This story I really have not heard," said Momma.

"When is he coming?" Herman asked. "Today?"

"Today? Don't forget about the Atlantic Ocean. It is a very big ocean," said Poppa. "It takes days and days to cross it and there are papers to sign when the ship arrives and identifications to show and at least a hundred delays. We will receive a notice from the authorities. Then

41

we will go to the authorities and bring Boris here. The authorities will notify us."

Poppa liked the word *authorities*. In these last few weeks Rachel had heard him say it frequently.

"Let me see your homework, Herman," Poppa said.

"It's too hard," said Herman. "The examples are too hard."

"I see a blank paper," said Poppa, shaking his finger at Herman. "Nothing was too hard for Boris when he was your age. When Boris comes, he will help you with your homework. There are tricks Boris knows, about how to find the right answers quickly. He would say to a whole group of us, children and adults, too, 'How much is 403 and 797 and 1204?' for example. 'Get pencils and paper and put those down,' he would say. And then add more long numbers. Then, while everyone struggled to add these up, he would say, 'Stop, I have given you enough time. I think the answer is,' let us say, '4,084,433. Is that correct?' Then someone would add all the numbers slowly, over and over, and we would see that he was right. Perhaps he will show you a way to do homework that will help you, too, to get the answers quickly."

"Maybe I won't have to learn the multiplication tables," said Herman, putting down his arithmetic homework.

"The multiplication tables come first," said Poppa, "then you can do the tricks. The tricks are built on the multiplication tables."

Herman was discouraged, but only for a little while. After he worked over his homework a while longer, he said, "Tricks? Can he do tricks, too? Can he make something vanish?"

"Not only vanish," said Poppa, "but reappear in some other form. Many, many tricks. You will see. Boris is a true magician."

But although Poppa talked confidently of Boris's coming any day, Rachel could see he was becoming more and more anxious over the delay in the arrival.

Poppa said one day, "Let's see, it takes fourteen days to cross the ocean. Allowing a week here and a week there and allowing for papers to be signed and for notices to be sent, we should nevertheless have heard from him."

"Perhaps he has come to visit some other relatives," said Momma. "Or to visit some friend first. Don't you think it is possible?"

"Impossible," said Poppa. "I know that the moment he arrives we will hear from the authorities."

Poppa looked over Herman's shoulder.

"Is eight times nine the same as nine times eight?" asked Herman.

"Yes," said Poppa. "Do you know the answer?"

"No. What's the answer?"

"Seventy-two. You have to say it five times," said Rachel.

"Seventy-two. Seventy-two. Seventy-two. Seventy-two. Seventy-two," said Herman fast.

"No," said Rachel. "You have to say five times: nine times eight is seventy-two. And then you must write it five times. You have to write the times eight table five times."

"The whole times eight table?" Herman said.

"Yes," Rachel said, "the whole table from one to twelve."

Herman began to write. It took him a long time to fill the blank sheet of paper.

"Now you will never forget it," said Poppa. "You will always remember that nine times eight is the same as eight times nine and that the answer is seventy-two. Do you know why? Because you will remember how you learned it. You will remember that one day we were speaking of Boris and that you asked a question of Rachel and this scene will remain in your memory forever and you will remember that eight times nine is seventy-two."

Rachel looked over Herman's shoulder. "No, you are writing it wrong. You are writing seventy-nine. Say it five more times, but say it right."

Herman tore up the sheet and began over again. He filled another sheet and wrote it right this time. Rachel stood beside him and then on another sheet she wrote,

$$6 \times 1 = 6$$
$$6 \times 2 =$$

"Now you must finish the times six table," said Rachel. "I began it for you . . . Miss Folsom is going to be surprised," she added.

After Herman wrote the times six table for a while he began to whisper to Rachel. "I went to Jimmy Johnson's house and I saw the kittens. One is orange and the other two are black and white."

"I wish we could have one," said Rachel, whispering too. "I wish we could have the orange one."

"The black and white are bigger. The orange one is the smallest."

Herman, instead of continuing with the times six table, was drawing a kitten on his arithmetic paper.

Rachel began the times five table for Herman on another sheet.

Poppa was saying in a low voice, "At first it was because of the summer. At least I thought so. But what about now? The summer is over. This bookstore of ours is still not well enough known. Yesterday the only people that came in were customers of Mr. Winkler's with watches to repair. I must admit I am disappointed."

"They are established here at school," said Momma, also in a low voice, "and we must wait a little while longer. We cannot move back and forth. When Boris comes, we will talk things over with him. You know how intelligent he is."

"For Boris this is a new country. We cannot tell Boris our problems. He will have his own. But I don't like to accept the bookstore space from Mr. Winkler any longer," said Poppa. "He is kind enough to wait for my business to improve, but he doesn't accept my share of the expense in the meantime."

"We are very fortunate to have Mr. Winkler to help us," said Momma. "Rachel," she went on, because Rachel had stopped watching Herman and was listening to them, "—Rachel, tomorrow we will move Herman's things into the parlor. We will change Herman's room into a room for Boris. Herman will sleep on the folding bed."

From the moment the letter had come, they had planned to make Herman's room into a room for Boris. Momma said that now, Rachel knew, because Momma didn't want her to hear that Poppa was disappointed in the bookstore. Momma didn't like him to feel disappointed, and especially didn't like Rachel to hear him say so.

5

The next day, just as Lizzie Stein was hurrying up the school steps in the morning, her arithmetic book dropped out of her other strapped books and fell at Rachel's feet. Rachel quickly stooped to pick it up and so did Lizzie, and as they stooped they banged their heads together.

They both laughed and held their aching foreheads.

Lizzie said, "Thank you, Rachel. I'm sorry I banged your head. Does it hurt?"

It did ache, but Rachel said, "Oh, no." She was very surprised. And then Lizzie said the most surprising thing of all.

"I suppose if we hadn't banged our heads together we'd never have talked to each other."

"I'm glad we did," Rachel said. She saw that Lizzie's face was brightest pink.

Rachel was just discovering something, and it made her very happy. Lizzie wasn't stuck-up at all, but she was very shy.

In the evening Herman told Poppa that Miss Folsom said he was the only one who knew the times seven table and the times eight table too. Miss Folsom, as a result, had put him into the first seat in the first row.

"You see," said Poppa, "you have been put into the first row and the first seat for one day. The question is, can you remain there?"

"Do the times six table," said Rachel. She wrote the first line on a sheet of paper for him once more. "If you know all the tables, you are going to stay in the first row."

"I went to Jimmy's house," said Herman, changing the subject. "Its eyes are open. Not the black and white ones. They're bigger, but their eyes aren't open. The orange one has his eyes open and they're blue. He said I could have it in two weeks. Jimmy's mother said I could have it in two weeks."

"You have to tell Jimmy that Momma won't let you have a kitten. And you have to tell him about the sign. Didn't you tell him about the sign?"

"Nope," said Herman. "What's the answer to six times seven?"

"Forty-two. Write it and then say it five times," said Rachel, thinking about an orange kitten, too, with a blue ribbon tied around its neck.

"If we had a mouse—" said Herman, whispering again, and looking up from the times six table.

"What?" said Rachel.

"Momma's afraid of a mouse," said Herman.

"I never saw one," said Rachel. "There aren't any in this house."

"What's six times seven?" said Herman.

"I just told you."

Momma came in with an armful of sewing. She sat near the table where Herman was doing his homework. Rachel was memorizing dates of the Civil War.

Momma unfolded a shirt of Herman's. A long ribbon of torn fabric fell away from it.

"Why is this new shirt torn?" asked Momma, holding up the shirt that Herman had worn when he went to get the cat out of the tree.

"It got caught," said Herman. "The shirt got caught on something."

"On what did it get caught? Did something reach out from somewhere and catch the shirt? Did a nail jump out of a wall? Or a doorknob reach out of a door to catch this shirt? Or—"

Suddenly Momma stopped. They all heard a tiny squeaking sound. Everyone looked at Momma. Momma was looking at the corner of the room near the icebox.

Momma said, "What do I hear?"

"Did you hear someone?" asked Poppa, looking up from his newspaper.

"I think it's a mouse," said Herman. "It sounded like a mouse."

Rachel stared at Herman, and Momma put her feet on the chair rung.

"Yes, a mouse," said Momma. "It sounded like a mouse. We will have to get a cat."

Herman jumped up. "I can get one," he said. "I know where to get a cat. It's in someone's house. It's a kitten, an orange-colored kitten."

"No," said Momma. "A kitten isn't enough for this mouse. This mouse sounds as if he could catch a kitten."

"Did you finish your homework?" said Poppa.

"Yes," said Herman. "It's finished. Can I get a cat?" He held up the sheet of paper entirely covered by the times six table. "I can get a cat instead of a kitten. I know where I can find a cat."

"Who can find a cat now? It's dark. We will have to wait until tomorrow." Then Momma looked again at the corner of the room.

"Suppose the mouse comes back?" said Herman. "And brings his whole family? And they climb all over us? All over the beds and the table and the pillows when we're asleep and all over the chairs and the sofa and—"

"Where can you find a cat," said Momma quickly, "in the middle of the night?"

53

"I know where there's a cat," said Herman, "a big cat. A black and white cat."

"Outside the delicatessen store," said Rachel.

"On Brook Avenue," said Herman.

"Rachel," said Momma, "go with Herman and see if they will lend us the cat for tonight. You can bring it back in the morning before you go to school."

"Come on, Rachel," said Herman. "Momma said we have to have a cat."

They hurried to Brook Avenue. There were occasional lighted windows and the street lamps were on, but most people had already gone to sleep. The avenue was tree-shadowed and quiet and the leaves in the light wind made the only sound beside their voices and footsteps.

Nine o'clock was the beginning of the evening Downtown, Rachel thought. All the lights in the stores would be on and people would be sitting on their stoops on chairs they brought out from their kitchens. People would be talking and laughing and calling down from windows to people downstairs and to people leaning out of other windows.

Kleinbaum's Delicatessen Store was open. Out-

side the store, as usual, a large black and white
cat sat washing his face.

Herman bent down and picked him up and
held him while Rachel went inside the store.

"Could we borrow your cat?" said Rachel.
"For tonight?"

"Take him, take him!" said Mrs. Kleinbaum.

"There are a hundred cats on this block." She peered at Herman, holding the cat just outside the doorway. "This one is a fighter."

Rachel said, "We'll bring him back in the morning."

But Mrs. Kleinbaum was talking to a customer who had asked for a pound of dried prunes.

"You will thank me for these prunes," said Mrs. Kleinbaum, weighing out the prunes and eating one herself.

As soon as Herman brought the cat home he crouched in front of the icebox.

"You see he knows why he is here," said Momma.

Rachel kneeled beside the cat and rubbed his head, which was smooth and silky. When she stopped, the cat lifted his head and rubbed against her hand. It was going to be hard to give him back to Mrs. Kleinbaum.

In the morning the cat came to Rachel and rubbed against her foot. Then he walked off a little way and went to Momma and rubbed his head against her foot, too.

56

"This cat has really frightened away the mouse," said Momma. "Herman, take him back to the delicatessen store on your way to school. Thank Mrs. Kleinbaum and tell her some other day we would like to borrow him if it is necessary."

"Let him stay one more day," said Herman. "Just for today let him stay here. I'll take him back in the afternoon."

"Positively no," said Momma.

The cat came to Momma again and rubbed against her foot.

"He knows about the fish," said Momma. "He knows there is a piece of fish for him in the icebox."

After the cat ate the fish, he spent a long time washing his face. Herman stood watching.

"Come on, Herman," said Rachel. "It's getting late."

"We'll borrow him again in a few weeks," said Momma. "He will remind the mouse in a few weeks that it is not safe here. Tell Mrs. Kleinbaum we'll borrow him another time."

"She doesn't want him," said Herman. "Nobody wants him. She wants to get rid of him. Someone else might take him for keep and then we couldn't borrow him any more."

"Take him back, Herman," said Momma, glancing at the clock. "Now you are late. I'll keep him until you come back. But only until you come back. In the afternoon you must take him back. Now go to school."

Rachel wanted to keep the cat, too. The whole house looked friendlier with a cat sitting in front of the icebox and washing his face. It was as if the cat belonged in their kitchen.

Because of the cat they hurried to get home from school.

"Maybe he can stay till tomorrow," said Herman. "Maybe Momma will hear the mouse again."

Rachel looked at Herman. A crowd had gathered at the corner of 149th Street and St. Ann's Avenue. Herman was trying to see what the crowd was looking at.

Some of the crowd left, and they saw an organ-grinder. He stood there, playing a sad, slow tune over and over. Herman went up close to him. A green, red, and yellow parrot was perched on a wire strung across the organ. Two other children came to stand beside Herman.

"He tells fortunes," one of the children said. "If you put down a penny, he'll pick out a card with your fortune on it."

No one had a penny.

The children looked at Herman, and Herman looked at Rachel, who shook her head. The parrot, tired of waiting for the penny, picked a worn card anyway out of a box of cards and held it out. The organ-grinder put it back into the card box. The crowd of children disappeared a few at a time and Rachel and Herman were the only ones left.

Rachel stood farther away than Herman because the parrot's claws frightened her. They were strong and sharp and restlessly went from one side of the wire to the other.

"Come on," said Rachel. "Come home. We have to take back the cat, Herman. Did you forget? Come on."

The first thing Momma said when they came home was, "The cat is gone. He must have run down the fire escape. One minute the cat is sitting at the open window beside the fire escape, and the next minute he is gone. I am sure he has gone home by himself. When a cat has a home he always finds his way back there."

Herman was already halfway out of the door.

60

"But if he has gone to the delicatessen store," Momma called after Herman, "don't bring him home. Remember, Herman—"

But Herman was on his way down the stairs.

Rachel went downstairs too. She walked around St. Mary's Park and slowly walked by the new Library. The scaffolding was down at last. A small sign at the door said the Library would be open on Friday. She thought of Becky Eisen. Becky loved to read and wanted to go with her to the Library Downtown any time Rachel wanted to go. She wished she knew someone like Becky who read a book a day. Shirley who lived next door loved to read, but her best friend was Katy Bloom and they went to Katy's Library, which was on Forest Avenue. Besides, Shirley was in 6B and all her friends were in 6B and 7A.

Walking home, Rachel went down Brook Avenue in order to pass Mrs. Kleinbaum's delicatessen store, just to see if the black and white cat had come home. An all-gray cat was asleep outside and another gray one was curled up beside the doorway. She was very sorry not to find the black and white cat. Overnight she had become attached to him.

In the early October afternoon Rachel walked home along St. Mary's Park. The trees were still as thickly leaved as in summer, but some of the leaves were beginning to turn orange and red. St. Mary's Park was the best part of living Uptown.

Someone called, "Rachel—Rachel—" She turned and there was Lizzie Stein hurrying to catch up.

"I just came to see when the Library would open," Lizzie said, "and there's a sign up that says Friday."

"I know. I saw it too," Rachel said, very glad to see Lizzie.

"My old Library is so far from my house I've been coming to find out about this one. Are you going to this one when it opens?"

"Oh yes, I've been waiting for it to open, too," Rachel said.

"I could call for you. Any time. I love to go to the Library. I always go on Friday afternoons."

"I do, too."

62

"Next Friday?" Lizzie said.

Rachel nodded.

"I could walk you home now," Lizzie said. "And then I'd know where to call for you."

Suddenly Rachel was very happy. Her wish was coming true. A minute before she had been wishing for a library friend, and now Lizzie was walking her home and was going to call for her next Friday. She didn't have to ask Lizzie if she'd be her friend, as the children used to ask each other Downtown. It was like having a friend already. No, it wasn't *like* having a friend. It was *really* having one.

"Do you ever go for long walks?" Rachel asked. "I love to take long walks."

"We could explore the Bronx," Lizzie said.

"Some Saturday?"

"Yes, let's."

"Where can Herman be?" said Momma when Rachel came home. "He went out and hasn't come back, not even to ask for a penny. Where can he be?"

63

Mrs. Glazer knocked and came in. "Would you happen to have an onion?"

"Take two," said Momma. "You haven't seen Herman?"

"You don't know where my son David and your son Herman are? They went to look for a cat. Herman told David you had a cat and the cat was lost and Herman said he had to find him because you are afraid of mice. I am afraid of mice, too," said Mrs. Glazer. "So, when your cat is found perhaps you will be good enough to let me borrow him. Just for a day or two. I thought I heard a mouse the other evening. While Herman and David were playing in my house, I thought I heard a mouse."

"Of course," said Momma, gladly promising to lend Mrs. Kleinbaum's lost cat. "Right now the cat is not at home, but of course—"

"Thank you very much," said Mrs. Glazer, "for the onion and for the cat, also."

There was a scratching sound.

"A mouse here too?" Mrs. Glazer said, looking alarmed.

Rachel went into the parlor. "It's the cat," she said.

They all came into the parlor. In the fading light they saw outside the window and sitting on the window sill the black and white cat, patiently scratching against the wood frame of the window.

"He wants to come in," said Mrs. Glazer. "Look how your cat wants to come in."

Rachel raised the window and in he came, as if he had been coming in through this very window all his life. The cat jumped down into the room and rubbed his head first against Rachel's foot and then against Momma's.

Momma was feeding him a saucer of milk when Herman hurried in.

Herman's hands and face were streaked with dirt. He looked hot, and his hair hung over his forehead.

"I looked into cellars and on roofs and I went into the park even—" Then Herman saw the cat. As if he were happily dreaming, Herman stood looking at the cat.

Rachel said, "He came back. The window was closed, so he scratched on it and waited until we let him in. He came up the fire escape."

"He lives here," said Herman. "Momma said a cat comes home. Here's where his home is. We have a trained cat."

Poppa came in. Momma told him, too, how the cat had gone out and returned home.

Poppa nodded as if he had always known this was an exceptionally intelligent cat.

"I can teach him tricks," said Herman. "I bet I can teach this cat to jump over a stick."

Poppa said, "He knows the trick of chasing a

66

mouse and of going out and coming back. He knows the trick of washing his face. Isn't that enough? How is the homework today?"

"I haven't done it yet," said Herman. "I'm just beginning."

"With those hands?" said Momma. "Look at your hands."

"All right," said Poppa. "I will wait. I will ask you later about the homework."

"Anyway," said Herman, "the cat can sleep with me. I can train this cat to sleep on my bed."

"I do not call this training a cat," said Poppa severely. "To train a cat you must train him *not* to sleep in a bed."

Momma had made the quince jam. She had polished the brass candlesticks even more brightly than usual. She had washed and ironed the curtains for the third time since Boris's letter had come. Every day for the last week she had said, "Something tells me that Boris is coming today. If it isn't today," she would add, "it will surely be tomorrow."

Today, late in the afternoon, she was washing

the kitchen floor, although it had been thoroughly washed the day before yesterday.

Everything was moved into a corner of the room and piled high, chairs on table and chairs on other chairs. Momma put on a big apron. Rachel put one on, too. Herman piled his own furniture in his room and Poppa directed him. Herman's room was going to be Boris's.

The floor was wet and shining with soapsuds, and the sun slanting into the window made tiny rainbows on the soap bubbles.

"Stay in the bedroom, Herman," said Momma, "until this floor is dry. If you walk on it now it will be covered with your footprints. It will have to be washed all over again."

A moment later there was a loud double knock and almost at once someone outside flung the door open.

"Boris—Boris is here!" Momma said, as if she did not believe her eyes.

Boris remained standing in the doorway. As if a magician had produced him out of thin air he stood there, sharing the surprise of his audience and smiling a wide, happy smile of triumph.

6

Boris looked like a friendly, white-toothed giant.
His hat was round and tall and made of black,
tightly curled fur, and he wore it tilted to one
side. His coat was long and black and had a collar
of the same black curly fur as his hat. In one hand
Boris held a large suitcase and in the other a polished black square case.

He stood there and then set down his luggage,
and rushed into the room, his coat flying open.

His coat, they all saw, was lined with fur, pale and brown.

"Boris!" Poppa said. "It is Boris! Boris, have you really arrived?"

"Can it be?" said Momma. "Can it really be you?"

"Why not? You don't recognize me? Boris? Boris Lessing?" He said it all in English and thumped his chest. Then he rushed at Momma and lifted her off the floor and kissed her and set her down again. Then he stared at Rachel. "Tell me who is this? Tell me at once who is this beautiful girl like a princess? Can this be Rachel?"

Suddenly Rachel, too, was swept off the floor and into the air, high above the fur hat.

"Take off your coat. Take off your coat and your hat. You must be warm. Let us look at you, Boris. How are you?"

Poppa was embraced by Boris, too, but Herman was given the most enthusiastic greeting. Boris clapped him on his shoulders and pretended to be unable to lift him off the floor. Then he put his own tall fur hat on Herman.

"You are so different," Momma said. "The same, and yet so, so—important-looking. Larger in width, taller in height—"

Poppa said, "And you speak such beautiful English."

"I am not different, I assure you," said Boris, continuing to speak in English, "here inside." And he thumped his chest again. "I am the same small boy you remember. Taller, older, that is all."

Poppa was helping him take off his long, fur-lined coat. Herman at last removed Boris's hat, which Boris had clapped on Herman's head. He examined it and then laid it carefully on the table's edge.

Boris stood in the very center of the glistening floor of soapsuds. Leading back to the door behind him were large, dark footprints.

Poppa began to pull down chairs. Everyone helped to set them about in a circle.

"Where shall we begin?" said Boris. "It has been many long years since we have seen each other."

71

"First of all, let me make tea," Momma said. "We must have tea if we are going to talk. And quince jam."

"Quince jam?" said Boris. "Now I know I am home again."

Momma moved quickly. She hurried the kettle on to the kitchen range and hurried plates on to the table.

"No, my dears, I am absolutely unchanged," said Boris. "I have seen the world. That is all. I have been in Paris. I have been in London, and now I am here in New York. I will tell you a big secret. This is the most wonderful and the best of all the cities I have seen. Why? Because *you* are all here."

Momma was about to cry. "Boris is the same. He can always make me laugh," she said.

Poppa said, "But why no letter? We expected to have a letter from the authorities to tell us you had arrived. We would have come to call for you wherever you were. Doubtless you were delayed."

"But why bother you?" said Boris. "I speak English. I can find my way. I have already traveled in the subway. I have seen the whole city of New

York. I have seen libraries, courthouses, schools, and I have seen the Woolworth Building."

Rachel thought of Downtown. It was a good thing Boris hadn't seen them in their old, crowded house. At least they were now established Uptown, and had Improvements.

"I have visited the theatres of New York," said Boris. "As you know, my life is the theatre. And I have seen Downtown. Downtown, my friends, there is an atmosphere of activity. There is noise, liveliness, crowds. It is strange, but I love crowds."

Cousin Boris had been here only a short time and already he noticed how quiet it was Uptown. Rachel, too, saw that she loved activity, noise, liveliness, and crowds.

Boris said, "First of all, I have some small presents for you. Because, my dears, thousands of miles away from you, I thought of you. These small presents are my thoughts of you, thousands of miles away from you."

Boris opened the large valise.

"Something for Rachel," he said, reaching inside and bringing out a package wrapped in red paper. Rachel opened it while everyone looked

73

on. She unwrapped from the red, crackling paper a large egg made of wood and painted like a fat little lady with a wide, smiling, fat, dimpled face and a shawl around her head and shoulders. The egg-shaped lady divided in half, top and bottom, and when opened there was a slightly smaller egg-shaped lady inside, and inside of her a smaller one. Eight egg-shaped ladies in all, and the smallest of them still fat and smiling and dimpled.

"And something else, too, before we are through with Rachel," said Boris. From inside

the valise, Boris lifted out a wide, flat box. Red satin roses were pressed into its cover and it was tied with red satin ribbons.

"Candy," Boris said, "from thousands of miles away."

"Let me see," said Herman.

But now something that occupied almost all the rest of the large valise was being helped out. "We must not forget Herman," said Boris, slowly drawing out a drum. Red and gold designs were painted on it, and the drumsticks were painted gold, too.

Herman, overjoyed with his gift, began at once to beat the drum.

"Herman has an ear for rhythm," Boris said. "He is musically talented."

Boris, making further searches in his valise, brought out a little cape of the fur his own hat was made of, and gave it to Momma.

Then Boris turned to Poppa. "Do you still have the silver watch that you won for excellence in fencing when you were in the Army?"

"I have it," said Poppa, reaching into his vest pocket.

"Then you will need this." And Boris took out of thin paper wrappings a thick silver chain.

"Beautiful. Exactly what I have wanted. But the watch was given to me not for fencing. Only for marksmanship," Poppa said modestly. Thick and heavy, the watch lay in the palm of his hand.

Poppa put the chain through a buttonhole and there it was, in two loops across his vest.

Momma was trying on her cape, Herman was beating his drum, and Rachel was opening the candy box. It was filled with little, hard red candies in the shape of raspberries.

"Before anything else," said Cousin Boris, "because we are all together and we are happy, we must have a little music." As he said that, Boris was unclasping the polished black square box he had carried in.

"The drum can wait, Herman," Boris said. "Now we will sing and play without drum accompaniment."

Out of its case Boris lifted the most beautiful of musical instruments, a black accordion inlaid with mother-of-pearl.

"But where are your things, all your clothing,

and your belongings?" Momma said. "I see only presents for us and an accordion."

"Did you think I would move into your house? Of course not. I have already brought my things to a hotel."

"A hotel?" said Momma, astonished. "Have you become a millionaire?"

"Not yet," said Boris. "Perhaps, in time, this too can happen. Who knows?"

Momma and Poppa stared at Boris, believing anything now. If Boris said that in time he would perhaps become a millionaire, it was like saying it was already a definite thing.

"The music will recall Chernovinsk to you, where we were all young. The days that we remember together, those days that are gone forever." Boris sighed, and Momma's eyes filled with tears.

The accordion in Boris's hands stretched out and then narrowed, and as a consequence it was suddenly as if a large orchestra had filed into the room . . . as if a hundred musicians had crowded into their top-floor apartment and were playing for them.

Boris sat on a kitchen chair and drew out the accordion slowly, and a sad song filled the air. Then he raised his voice.

Dark beautiful eyes, sang Boris. *Beautiful dark eyes.*

"Play some more," Poppa urged him, when Boris stopped.

"Play, play," said Momma.

"This one is for Rachel. It is about a little bird that flies away from a little girl," said Boris. "The little girl is sad. When the little bird observes this, he flies back to her. She is happy." Boris played a lively song.

The more he played, the more beautiful it seemed to Rachel and the prouder she was of Cousin Boris. More than anything she longed to open the door wide so that their neighbors could hear the music too, and would know that it came from their house. Boris played song after song. He sang all the words, and they were in half a dozen languages. She would learn all the languages Cousin Boris knew, Rachel was thinking. She would have to learn the words and what they meant and then she would sing them too.

"Now," said Boris. "Here is a song of the sadness of falling leaves. Then comes winter. Very, very sad. Then comes springtime and light-heartedness."

"Beautiful," said Poppa, shaking his head in wonder.

Herman, as if enchanted, sat motionless, watching Boris play the accordion.

"I will play a little dance for Herman. A sailor's dance. You remember this dance?" Boris asked Poppa. "I will teach it to you, Herman, and then you can teach it to your school friends and all your friends can dance it too when they are happy."

Boris began to play a lively tune, and a wonderful thing happened. He stood up and then, still playing, bent his knees; his legs began to shoot out from his body as if they were on taut wire. And through it all he kept time to the happy music he played.

"Rest a little," said Momma to Boris. "You will tire yourself out."

"I am not tired," said Boris.

The music was at its loudest and the dancing at its liveliest when three loud bongs came from the radiator pipes.

"You see," said Boris, shouting over his music and his dancing, "others wish to join our concert."

"You must be tired," said Momma, "and downstairs they are tired too, and we are keeping them from going to sleep. Some people are not so musical as others."

Herman, from being hypnotized by the music and the dancing, came to life. "How do you do that?" he said. "How do you dance like that?"

"It's easy. When I was your age, I was already

celebrated as a dancer of this dance. You want to learn, Herman? Look. First you bend your knees." Boris showed Herman how to bend his knees and how to balance his body. "Now, as you are not yet playing an accordion, you fold your arms across your chest. I see you are a born dancer of this dance." Boris played and Herman began to dance and to fall over. Herman danced all around the room, falling frequently.

"Certain things," Poppa said, "Herman learns very fast. Like this dance."

Three more bongs were heard from the radiator pipes.

"Let us have tea now," said Momma, standing up. "Boris, yours will be in a glass, as you like it."

Momma poured the tea into a tall glass and set out the quince jam she had made for Boris.

"Yes," Boris said, putting his accordion into its case. "It is like Life. Just as we begin to talk, what happens? We see it is too late. I too must prepare for tomorrow. Tomorrow I begin to work at the theatre."

"Are you now an actor?" Momma said.

"No, my dear, not an actor. A designer. The theatre is my world. I live for the theatre."

"Is it true?" Poppa said, surprised.

"Today I have seen a theatre. That is to say, I have seen a bare, ugly stage. 'If you want me to work here,' I say to the manager, 'you must order a hundred yards of green velvet, at least one hundred yards. No, red is better. I will have to work in more beautiful surroundings than these.' Tomorrow the velvet will be there and I will begin."

"I want to see a theatre," Herman said. "Rachel and I want to go to see a theatre."

Rachel looked at Herman and was grateful to him. The more Cousin Boris described the theatre, the more she wanted to see it.

"You shall. All of you shall see my theatre. Only wait until I have finished my work properly. Wait until the play is produced. You shall all go and see the play. After I have cut the red velvet and designed a proper setting and installed a proper curtain, et cetera, I will come to you with the invitation. This theatre will be magnificent!"

"Where is it?" asked Poppa.

"Downtown," said Boris.

"Downtown is very big," said Poppa. "Where Downtown?"

"On Second Avenue," said Boris. "But you must wait until I will come and take you there myself. Then I shall show all of you my designs and my settings, et cetera. We will continue our music tomorrow. Today I have played for Herman. To-

83

morrow I will play songs only for Rachel. Meanwhile I leave the accordion with you."

"The accordion is safe with us," said Poppa.

"We will talk and sing again tomorrow. Now I leave you. I leave you and you and you and you. And you, too, beautiful cat," he said, bending over Mrs. Kleinbaum's cat. The cat had hidden himself because of the accordion music and the dancing. Now he had come out and was lying in front of the icebox.

"This is a fine cat," said Boris, studying him. "What is his name?"

"So far," said Momma, "he has no name."

"No name? How can you have an animal without a name in the house? How do you call him?"

"We don't have to call him," said Herman. "He's right here except when he's out."

"But when he is out," said Boris, "and you want him to come in, what do you do?"

"We leave the window open," said Herman.

"Nevertheless," said Boris, "this cat should have a name. Once we had a cat named Peter the Great. Do you remember the black cat named Peter the Great?" Boris asked Poppa.

84

"It was long ago," said Poppa, "but I remember that cat very well. Peter the Great is suitable for this cat also."

"Absolutely suitable," Boris said. "Until tomorrow, then."

"Until tomorrow."

Rachel looked at Mrs. Kleinbaum's cat. Giving him the name of Peter the Great seemed to change him altogether. He looked more dignified now, and his head was shining as if polished. "Peter the Great," she called to him softly. "Peter the Great!" But it was as if he hadn't heard. He neither looked up nor moved. She would have to call him Peter the Great until he knew his name. "Peter," she called. "Pete!" When she had called him six times he looked up and yawned. He's tired, Rachel thought, and so am I. Tomorrow I must teach him his name.

7

Rachel could hardly get up in the morning. It seemed to her she had just fallen asleep when she heard the alarm. She heard other sounds, too. She heard Herman practicing the dance he had learned from Cousin Boris and singing the song about the little bird.

Herman was very happy on the way to school.

"I know all the multiplication tables," said Herman, "up to nine."

"I'll write the times nine table for you this

afternoon," said Rachel. "Then you can stay in the first seat in the first row."

"Poppa says Boris can do tricks. I want to see him make something vanish tonight."

"Better do the times nine table, Herman. If Boris stays as late as he stayed last night, you'll never get your homework done."

Herman stopped walking. "Wait," said Herman. "Is four times nine the same as nine times four?"

"Yes. Come on."

"I know the times nine table, too. Because I know the times two and the times three and all the way up to times eight, and nine is in all the tables. Listen," Herman said. "One times nine is nine. Two times nine is eighteen. See, Rachel?"

"Better write it five times," Rachel said, but she was proud of Herman for discovering the times nine table in the others.

"I know all except the last of it without writing it," said Herman. Herman was so happy over unexpectedly discovering the times nine table that he danced a few steps of Boris's dance on the way to school.

In Rachel's classroom, Miss Bannerman read a list of people who needed help in arithmetic. Gladys Mahoney was one.

"Everyone who needs help," said Miss Bannerman, "may choose a partner for homework from the list on the blackboard."

Rachel looked up. Six names were written on the blackboard. She was surprised to see that the name after Tom Donahue was Rachel Lessing.

Gladys said, "I choose Rachel Lessing. If she'll have *me*."

"Would you do your homework once or twice a week with Gladys, Rachel?"

Rachel nodded quickly. "Yes, ma'am."

George Davis chose Tom Donahue, and four others chose the remaining four.

"The trouble is," Rachel said to Gladys later, "I have a brother."

"I have no brothers or sisters," said Gladys. "Can you come home with me? Would you be allowed?"

"I'll ask," said Rachel. "I have to ask."

When Rachel asked if she could go to Gladys's

house, Momma said, "But you must come home before dark. This is not Downtown."

"I'll come home before dark."

"It's dark already," said Herman. "What time is it?"

"Half-past seven," said Momma, looking out of the window. "It's the middle of the night."

"I'll come back at half-past five," Rachel promised.

"When is Boris coming?" said Herman. "I want to see some tricks. I've finished all the examples." Herman held up a sheet covered with homework.

Rachel looked it over. "Everything looks right."

"Boris will be here, you may be sure. Are you still in the first seat in the first row?" Poppa asked.

"Nope," said Herman. "I was put in the last seat because I was showing someone the dance that Boris showed me. I was just showing Jimmy the dance and Jimmy and Tony and some other boys were learning it and Miss Folsom saw me. She said I was noisy. Here's a note you have to sign," Herman added. "Miss Folsom said you have to sign it. I have to bring it back to her." He gave the note to Poppa.

Dear Mr. Lessing,
    Herman has a whistle that sounds like a mouse squeaking. Please see to it that he does not bring it to school again. Please sign this.

                Yours truly,
                Mary Folsom

Poppa shook his head at Herman, then looked at the cat near the icebox.

"Ah-ha," said Poppa, but he did not tell Momma about the whistle.

"On the way home I saw the man with the polly and the music, but he hasn't got the polly any more," Herman said, looking away from Poppa and at Rachel.

There was a ring of the doorbell.

"Here's Boris," said Herman, running to the door.

It was Mr. Feeney. "Your mother home, Herman?"

"What is it?" said Momma, coming to the door, too.

"I was looking up from the yard the other day and I see a cat coming out of your window, Mrs. Lessing," said Mr. Feeney.

"A cat?" said Momma, her face getting pink. "What kind of a cat?"

"Your cat," said Mr. Feeney, looking at Momma in surprise. "Your black and white cat. I see it a couple of times. Can I have a loan of that cat if you don't mind? For the basement?"

"What's in the basement?" said Momma, trying to hide her embarrassment.

"Mice," said Mr. Feeney. "Maybe rats."

"We have mice in the basement? You are welcome to this cat," said Momma. "He comes and he goes. Take him."

"Don't you worry. I'll bring him right back myself," said Mr. Feeney. "Tomorrow morning." He walked into the kitchen and picked up Peter the Great from in front of the kitchen range, just as Herman had done in front of Mrs. Kleinbaum's store. The cat seemed as pleased to be carried away by Mr. Feeney as by Herman.

Boris arrived at eight o'clock.

He took off his warm coat and hat. "I have been working hard. Measuring, cutting, arranging. Tomorrow it must be finished. Tomorrow it *will* be finished. I will see later about lights and settings. During the rehearsal."

"Lights, settings, rehearsals. It is another world," Poppa said in wonder and astonishment.

Momma said nothing. She sat there as Herman sat, staring at Boris. Then she said, "To think you are really here, and already so worried about the theatre. Even understanding all this is difficult for us."

Rachel agreed with Momma and with Poppa. It was another world and it was hard to understand, but she could see it all, full of lights and red velvet. It would be wonderful to be allowed to see it really. Boris had promised to take them all. She could hardly wait. And she could hardly wait to tell Lizzie Stein about it afterward.

"Ah, understanding," Boris was saying. "This is the only important thing. There is one man, however, whose name I will not mention. He is always saying, 'But do you need so much material? Do you really need to spend all that?' One thing I do not like is petty economy."

"Can you do magic?" Herman said. "Poppa says you can do tricks. Do a trick, Boris."

"Boris can do anything," said Momma. "Tricks are the least."

"One trick only," Boris said. "Don't forget, tomorrow is a day for working. It is not a day for sleeping. And for you, Herman, it is a school day. Am I right?"

"Yes, you are right," said Poppa. "One trick, however, Herman should be allowed to see. One will be enough."

"Very well, I will show you a trick. But for this piece of magic I will ask you to bring me a knife, an ordinary butter knife or a dull kitchen knife. It doesn't matter, even an old, useless one will do."

Herman hurried out, and returned at once with a butter knife.

"First I wash my hands," said Boris. "When I return you will examine my hands and my arms and you will see they are newly washed. You will also see I conceal nothing."

When Boris came back, he said, "Now, my dear ones, examine my hands and my arms. Examine my sleeves. Examine the knife also."

They all felt his hands and arms, his sleeves and the knife.

Herman rolled down Boris's sleeves, which had been rolled up, and then rolled them up again.

"It is true. Nothing is concealed," said Poppa.

"Now examine the knife," offered Boris. "Carefully examine the knife."

It was an ordinary butter knife. They had all seen it a thousand times. Except Boris. Now it was passed from hand to hand and carefully examined as if it were something new and strange.

"We are well acquainted with this knife," said Poppa, returning it to Boris.

"Good," said Boris, grasping the butter knife by its handle as if it were a dagger and holding it point downward. "I want everyone to know that this butter knife will soon drip water."

"It'll drip *water?*" asked Herman.

"Yes," said Boris, "but to make sure it is perfectly dry at this moment, look at it once more."

Again it was passed from hand to hand. Everyone saw it was dry.

"Dry it off with a towel," commanded Boris.

Rachel ran for a towel and dried the butter knife thoroughly, as if it were wet.

"Now," said Boris, again grasping the knife and raising it high above his head. "Now we shall see if I am able by means of magic to cause this butter knife to drip water." Again he held it point downward. "Now, look closely at the table where I have placed a saucer. In a moment some drops of water will drip from this knife. At least, this is what I hope."

They all leaned forward, staring at the saucer.

Slowly Boris lowered his hand, very slowly brought it down from above his head, then held the knife directly over the saucer. Gripping it tightly, Boris said, "This is a difficult knife to get water from. But I will try." He grasped the knife even more tightly.

No one made a sound or moved. Then from the point of the knife a drop of water slowly fell into the saucer. Then another, a third, and a fourth. At the bottom of the saucer there lay a tiny pool of water.

Boris, flushed and happy, smiled his wide, white-toothed smile. "And here is your knife," he said, giving it back to Herman.

The knife was still damp.

"Do it again," said Herman. "Let me see you do it again."

"One trick only," said Poppa. "We agreed on one trick only."

"We must let Boris rest," said Momma. "To-morrow Boris must work in the theatre, cutting and rehearsing and so forth."

"Instead of doing a trick, I will play a little for you on the accordion," said Boris. "I will play a lullaby for Herman, and a little song for Rachel. Herman will go to sleep. And I will go home."

Boris played the lullaby on his accordion. Rachel passed the red candies that Boris had brought, and ate a few herself while Boris played the song for her and a second and third one.

Boris stood up at last. "Now I must leave you and you and you and you."

"Tell me how you do it, Boris. How do you do the knife trick?" Herman asked.

"When you are twenty-one I will tell you. It is a trick that can only be learned if you are twenty-one years old."

Herman was quiet. It was a great effort for Herman to do mental arithmetic. Then he had it. "It's only twelve more years. That's all."

"That's all," said Boris. "Twelve more years. You will turn around once or twice and it is twelve years later. We can do this on the stage simply by lowering and raising the curtain."

"By magic?" said Herman

"True magic," Boris said. "I shall see you. I shall see you before you have had time to recover from my visit, and long before you are twenty-one years old, Herman. Sleep well. Tomorrow we shall have a long and happy evening after my work is done." He kissed them all. "I am leaving the accordion, as before."

"Of course," said Momma. "We will take care of it."

8

It had been hard for Rachel to get up after Boris's first visit, but the morning after his second visit she could not get up at all. She turned her head into her pillow when the alarm rang out.

From the next room she heard Momma say, "Get up, Rachel. Do you know what time it is? It is time to leave and you are not even out of bed."

Inside Rachel's head were visions of a tall fur hat and a long fur coat, of lively dancing, of loud singing, of an accordion that played by itself, and of drops of water running out of a knife. There was a disturbing feeling in her stomach of red candies as indestructible and heavy as small red rocks.

"In a minute," she called back to Momma. "I'll be up in a minute."

But perhaps she only thought she was saying that.

"Why don't you answer, Rachel?" Momma said, hurrying to the side of Rachel's bed. "You must be sick. It seems to me you are sick." Momma was bending over Rachel and putting her hand to Rachel's head.

Instead of telling Rachel to hurry and to get up, Momma said quietly, "Go to sleep again, Rachel. Herman will go to school by himself today."

As soon as Momma said that, Rachel sat up quickly, or thought she would try to sit up. "I must go to school today," she said to no one at all, as Momma had already gone back into the kitchen. "There's a test. An arithmetic test. Miss Bannerman—" Rachel saw the whole room swing around slowly as if to Boris's sad accordion music.

"Herman, go to school by yourself. Rachel stays at home today. Too many red candies," said Momma, quickly coming to the point.

Rachel slid under the covers again. The room stopped dancing. Her eyes were shut. Behind their closed lids she could still see Boris dancing and playing, but more faintly. She could see the accordion stretch out wider and wider and hear it play louder and louder and then become smaller and smaller, until at last it disappeared altogether and was quiet.

She fell asleep. It seemed to Rachel she slept for a long time. Then when she woke up Momma was talking in a low voice to someone in the kitchen.

"We must have a little more patience," Momma said, "but I too am worried. It is better for the children here, Uptown, and we have Improvements. You can see how much better it is. The streets are wide and the park is close. I would be ashamed to move Downtown again after moving Uptown."

"So, well, all right." Rachel recognized Aunt

Riva's voice. "I have saved up some money. Please take it. When things get better you will repay me."

"Never, positively never," Momma said. "We still have some savings left, and we haven't talked to Boris yet. He is full of ideas. Riva, will you stay to meet him? He is lonely. Although he seems happy, remember he is alone here, after all. He should meet other young people, Riva. I think he should meet you."

Rachel sat up in bed. Of all her aunts, Momma's sister, Riva, was her favorite. Riva was like someone her own age. She was lively and loved to laugh and play with Rachel and with Herman. Rachel loved to look at Riva, who had soft, dark hair and large, dark eyes.

"Aunt Riva, Aunt Riva, is it you?" Rachel called.

"Are you better, Rachel?" Aunt Riva came running in.

"All better—I think." The room no longer sailed around her, and her stomach no longer felt weighed down by red candies.

"So, well, all right, come on, hurry up," Aunt

Riva said. All these words she said in English quickly. She used them frequently, and interspersed them throughout her speech. *Anyhow* was her great favorite. She used *anyhow* whether it was suitable or not.

She helped Rachel dress, buttoning her up in the back and patting the skirt straight. "All right," she said, "well, anyhow."

They went into the kitchen arm in arm. Momma was cutting up potatoes into a large iron pot.

"Riva, as long as Rachel is at home, stay. Later on Boris will come, too. You must hear his songs and his stories. We haven't even begun to talk. Don't forget we haven't seen Boris in years. He must have hundreds of stories to tell us."

"Please," said Riva suddenly, as if she hadn't been listening to a single word Momma was saying, "I am going to ask everybody a favor. Everybody please call me Rose. No more Riva."

Momma looked at Riva and said, "What does it matter, Riva or Rose? If you like Rose better, of course we will call you Rose." Momma looked at her to see how her new name suited her. "Riva is a nice name. Rose is a nice name. If you want to be Rose, all right."

"Yes, I do want to," Riva said. She paused a moment and looked at Rachel. "It is better to be Americanized. Anyhow, well, so, we are in America now. Not in Chernovinsk. So, well, all right, here our names should be American names and we should try to talk this new language. *So, come on, we'll talk in English.*" She had said the whole last sentence in English. Momma stopped cutting up the potatoes and looked at her with pride.

"One, two, three," said Momma, "and you have taught yourself English. And Boris too. You are both alike in learning quickly and in speaking English. Riva—I mean Rose—stay."

"No," said Aunt Rose. "It would be better if he would call me up."

" 'Call me up?' What does it mean, 'Call me up'?"

"I have a telephone now."

"You have a *telephone?*"

"Well, anyhow," said Aunt Rose, "it's downstairs. In the candy store. I will leave you the number."

"Positively no," said Momma. "It is better to meet in your own relatives' house. How does it look to 'call you up' in some strange candy store?"

"All right, so, I will tell you what I will do," said Aunt Rose, as if she had thought it out in advance. "I will come in two weeks. Sunday morning, a week from next Sunday, because next Sunday I already have an appointment. If you like, ask your Boris to come Sunday morning and we will all go for a walk."

There was a little mirror at the back of the sideboard in the dining room, and while Rose was saying this she was looking at herself. Then she turned to Rachel. "Come here, Rachel. I think I see a resemblance between us."

"I wish I did look like you," Rachel said, looking at Rose's shining dark eyes and lovely hair.

"You two look like sisters," Momma said. "The same eyes. The same little nose."

And suddenly Rachel could see it too, just as Momma said. It made her very happy. Aunt Rose bent and kissed the top of Rachel's head. It pleased Aunt Rose, too, to see the resemblance between them.

"On Sunday we'll go Downtown," Aunt Rose said. "We'll walk across the new bridge. Or else we can go to Bronx Park."

"What new bridge do you mean?" Momma asked.

"Don't you know the new bridge on Delancey Street?"

"This bridge has been standing there for at least ten years," said Momma.

"For me," said Rose, "it is a new bridge. I haven't yet walked across it."

"I have seen the bridge," said Momma, "but I have never seen Bronx Park."

"All right, so," said Aunt Rose, "we can all go

to Bronx Park. I will walk with someone else on the bridge. Now I must leave. I will have to go to the factory to see if there is any work for this afternoon." She began to go toward the door, but turned back. "Anyhow, you won't say I—made this suggestion about meeting Boris."

"Of course not," said Momma. "You will simply come to visit us as Boris will. Besides, we are all relatives. We should all know each other better."

9

Rachel walked home with Gladys Mahoney the next day. It had rained and all the streets were wet and shining. The leaves shook down little showers of wetness, too, as they walked along St. Mary's Park. They passed Kleinbaum's and walked away from Rachel's neighborhood of apartment houses and stores.

On Gladys's street all the houses were red brick and two stories high. Trees in even rows lined both sides of the street. In front of each house there was a square of clipped grass, and along the sidewalk and dividing each neat grass plot from its neighbor there was a low, black iron picket fence.

"This is where I live," said Gladys, in front of one house in the middle of the block. Except for an enormous rubber plant beside the door it was exactly like its neighbors on either side. Gladys opened the low iron gate and they walked up the flagstone path to the front door.

"Let's go to my room," Gladys said.

Gladys's bed had a roof with a white ruffle around it, and the roof was held up by four thin, tall posts. Gladys's dresser had a round mirror in which the whole room and Gladys and Rachel were reflected. There were a high-backed rocking chair and a small armchair covered in flowered material. All of it was like the picture of a child's room in a book. Better than anything was a child's-size, red-painted table and two child's-size chairs. On the little table there was a lamp with a rose-patterned shade. When Gladys turned it on it bathed the whole room in a rosy light.

It took a long time to get to the homework—

first because Rachel could not stop staring at Gladys's picture-book room, and then because Gladys had a pencil sharpener that Rachel loved to use. It made beautiful points and also made long, curling shavings. All Gladys's pencils and Rachel's were half their former size after Rachel had used the pencil sharpener on them.

As Rachel was opening the Arithmetic, Gladys said, "Let's have cookies before we begin."

"Let's do our homework first," Rachel said. She had already spent far too much time on the pencil sharpener, and felt guilty about neglecting Gladys's homework.

"Just hot chocolate," Gladys said, "and a cookie." She called to her mother. "Can we have hot chocolate, Mother?"

"I must go home before it gets dark," Rachel said, "and we haven't even begun."

"We'll do our homework now, while we're waiting." Gladys began to write. She was something like Herman, Rachel saw. She had never written out multiplication tables and she was careless and added too quickly.

Rachel made Gladys write tables. "Write them

five times," she said, just as she had told Herman.

She had written out all of the homework examples when Gladys's mother came in. On a tray there were cookies and two blue and white china cups and saucers. When Mrs. Mahoney set down the tray, it reminded Rachel of the first Sunday after they had moved Uptown. Poppa had taken them to an ice-cream parlor and they had had exactly this: hot chocolate with floating whipped cream.

Gladys's mother said, "Hello, Rachel," and

smiled at her. She reminded Rachel of a teacher. She talked English like a teacher and she was tall and wore eyeglasses that caught shining lights; and she wore a white waist with ruffles down the front of it, just like those Miss Bannerman had on her white waist. She was altogether different from Momma, Rachel was thinking. Momma wore an apron most of the time except when she was expecting relatives. Momma said, "Lessing, let me borrow your eyeglasses," when she wanted to read the small print in the newspaper. Momma didn't talk English at all, or rather Momma didn't trust herself before strangers to speak the few words she knew of the new language.

It was harder and harder to pay attention to Gladys's homework. Rachel looked over Gladys's paper. Everything was neatly written and everything was right. And then her eyes were drawn to the hot chocolate and whipped cream.

"You don't need me to help you, Gladys. You know the times twelve table and it's the hardest one."

"I do know it," Gladys said thoughtfully. "Most of the time I know the answers when Miss

Bannerman asks me, but my attention wanders. I wish you'd pinch me, Rachel, when I stare out of the window at school. Especially on a nice day. I think about Saturday afternoons and Sundays and going out on the boat. That's when I get everything wrong."

"What boat?"

"We have a boat up at City Island," Gladys said. Then she looked anxiously and hopefully at Rachel. "Would you be allowed to come out with us sometime?"

"In a rowboat?"

"It's a motorboat and it has a cabin. My dad gets it going, sometimes anyway, and then we cruise up and down the Sound. Mostly we scrape and paint and shine up the brass. But it's fun."

Rachel was spellbound by the thought of a boat with a cabin, whatever that was.

"Mother," Gladys called through the door, "can Rachel come with us next Sunday? Out to the boat?"

Gladys's mother came in, looking more like a teacher than ever because now she had a book in her hand.

"Rachel's entirely welcome," Gladys's mother said. "We may even have a ride this Sunday."

"Will your mother let you come?" Gladys asked.

Positively no, Momma would say. Do you want to drown?

"I don't think so," Rachel said. "I get seasick, even on a train."

"It's not anything like a train. Ask, anyway, Rachel. See what your mother says. It doesn't hurt to ask. And be sure you tell her we have a million Life Preservers. Twelve, I think."

"I'll ask," said Rachel, her heart thumping against her ribs. "I'm dying to go on a boat. With a cabin."

The light in the sky was fading and the rain was falling again as a light mist in the air. It was like something beginning, strange and disturbing and new and wonderful. It's a new world, Poppa had said. He meant riding in boats with cabins with a girl like Gladys, who had a mother like a teacher. Gladys walked Rachel halfway home and then Rachel ran all the rest of the way.

"Positively no," said Momma. "Not on a boat. Do you want to drown?"

"They have Life Preservers. Twelve. Three for each person," said Rachel.

"If they have so many Life Preservers, there must be a great danger of drowning."

Poppa said, "One must see everything. Let Rachel see what a boat looks like. We ourselves came to America on a ship. Rachel has never even seen a small boat."

"If you go," said Momma, "promise me you will sit near the Life Preservers as long as you are on this boat."

Rachel ate her supper quickly while telling Momma about Gladys's bed with the ruffled roof, and the hot chocolate, and the little table with the lamp. Even Herman listened.

"It's a whole new world," said Poppa. "Uptown is a new world."

"Where could one meet such people Downtown," said Momma, "with boats and Life Preservers and hot chocolate and beds with roofs? I'll wash the blue and white dress. It looks like a new dress when I put plenty of starch in the water. It will be ready for Sunday."

"I can come," Rachel said. "I can come with you. My mother said I can come."

"I just knew it," Gladys said. "I just counted on it."

Rachel tried not to think of Sunday and the boat, but whenever she looked out of the window she, too, was like Gladys, imagining a sunny day with a boat she had never seen, on a blue sea.

"Wear old things," said Gladys, "so you won't get paint on your good things in case we're still painting. I guess Dad will still do *some* painting. I'll call for you. We have homework together on Thursday. We'll talk about it."

It was very difficult to keep her mind on arithmetic when they were going on the boat next Sunday.

Momma had already washed the blue and white dress with the sailor collar. It was her best dress and Rachel intended to wear it. She told Gladys.

"It doesn't matter," said Gladys. "We have old

clothes for you to wear. We keep all kinds of junk in our locker and then put them on when we go on the boat. You'll get splashed."

"It's four whole days to Sunday," Rachel said. "I wish we could go tomorrow."

"I always count the days too," Gladys said. "Now there are two of us."

Coming back from school next day, Rachel and Herman saw a little crowd and heard organ-grinder music. They made their way to the center of the crowd and then saw why there were more children than usual. Everyone was watching a little monkey sitting on the music box. The little monkey blinked and looked around at the crowd and took off his little hat and looked again.

Everyone watched the monkey. He wore a green hat that had a long, red feather, and the whole thing looked as if it had been out in the rain. The feather sagged and curled around the monkey's tiny body, which was dressed in a little red coat.

He took off his feathered hat every now and then and put it back with the greatest care, as if he knew it was valuable. And when he held out

the hat for pennies, he held out not his own feathered hat but one that the organ-grinder gave him for begging.

"I wish I had a monkey and a *Katrinka*," said Herman, using Momma's word for the music box. "I'd take him home and I'd train him to sleep in my bed and I'd train him to sit next to me while I did homework and he wouldn't have to beg."

"Come on," said Rachel. "Let's do our homework. When Boris comes, we'll be through with it. I'll help you. Come on."

"Wait a minute," said Herman.

The organ-grinder was beginning to walk while playing, but he was going in the opposite direction from home.

"Can we walk along one block?" Herman asked.

"No, we must go home. Come on."

"One half block?"

"Come on," said Rachel, taking Herman's hand and pulling him along toward home.

10

"If it rains we'll put it off until next Sunday," Gladys said. "My mother thinks you should come only if it's a sunny day."

It had never occurred to Rachel that it might rain. She watched the sky anxiously. It rained on Friday and her heart sank. But Saturday was clear and on Sunday the bright morning sun, shining into Rachel's room, woke her up. Not a single cloud could be seen in the deep blue sky.

"Stay close to the Life Preservers," said

Momma. "Don't catch cold. Here is your warm coat. The weather is altogether different on water."

Rachel went downstairs at nine o'clock. Her winter coat was over her arm. Momma had made enough sandwiches for Rachel and for Gladys, too, and for Gladys's mother and father. Momma had wrapped up the sandwiches and fitted them into a shoe box.

At two minutes after nine Gladys came running up the street. "Mother and Dad are waiting at the trolley stop on the corner." Gladys took the shoe box from Rachel and together they ran to the corner. "I overslept," Gladys said, "then I remembered you were coming and leaped out of bed. When I get on the boat I'll finish my sleep. You'll have to play with the dog while I sleep."

"A dog too? You have a dog?"

"It's the dock dog. I'll tell you about him when I'm not out of breath. He's Dad's friend."

"This is Rachel, Daddy, Rachel Lessing," Gladys said, still out of breath, as they came up to the Mahoneys.

Gladys's father said, "How do you do, Rachel," and shook hands with her as if she were grown up and as old as Momma or Poppa. "I'll take that," Mr. Mahoney said, putting Rachel's shoe box into a covered basket he was carrying. His face looked as if he had been out of doors in a windy, cold climate all his life. His hair was sandy brown and his eyes were bright blue.

They rode through miles of Bronx avenues and streets. Gladys and Rachel sat at the back of the trolley. Gladys's mother and father found seats at the front.

They traveled away from the neighborhood of the tall apartment houses and rode along fields and saw occasional small white houses scattered among the fields. Soon they could see in-and-out glimpses of water, and sails catching sunlight, and over all of it a deep blue, cloudless sky.

Now water replaced the land along one side of the trolley tracks.

"See all those boats?" Gladys said. "Our boat is one of that crowd."

It was a lovely sight. Boats of all sizes, with

sails and without, lay at anchor in the water. Some were docked at the edge of the water, and people were busily at work around them. Even little children were working on the boats.

"Last stop!" the trolley conductor called out.

"There—!" said Gladys. "I can see her from here."

They ran to the edge of the land. The biggest of the boats, white and gleaming in the sun, was the one Gladys was showing Rachel. *Anna Marie* was lettered on its side.

"It's a lovely name for a boat," said Rachel.

"It's my mother's name. Come on, let me show you inside."

Gladys was one of the quietest girls in school, but she was completely changed now. Here she was as restless and lively as Herman.

"Come on, Rachel," Gladys said, "come up on deck."

From what Gladys called the deck, Rachel looked down. They were on land, but only on one side. From the other it was a world of boats and water. Momma and Poppa and Herman seemed a million miles away, and it was a million more from Downtown and from all the familiar things she knew.

Momma and Poppa and Herman and the bookstore began gently to recede. Farther and farther. Only water and boats remained. Only seaside sounds and the slapping noise of the water against the nearby boats. Only she and Gladys were left of the old world she had known up to now.

Gladys's father in overalls came up, carrying a pail of white paint. The paint smell and the smell of the sea were mixed. Rachel watched Mr. Mahoney stir the paint. It seemed to her she was only half awake. In her half-awake state everything and everyone blurred and merged: Boris and Miss Bannerman, Mr. Mahoney and Mr. Winkler, the bookstore and the boat.

Boris had crossed the ocean and he had been in many countries, she was thinking. The world was enormous, full of little boats and big ones, of ocean and sky and Downtown and Uptown. Of people like Momma and like Mrs. Mahoney, of people like Boris and like Mr. Mahoney. Everyone was different. They might find each other strange, and maybe Momma wouldn't know enough English to talk to Mrs. Mahoney if she should meet her, but she, Rachel, didn't find any one of them strange. She could understand them all and talk to them all. It was funny that she, Rachel, not yet twelve years old, didn't find any one of them strange. They were all her friends. She closed her eyes and took a deep breath of the paint and sea smell.

"Are you asleep, Rachel?"

"Only half asleep. I love this smell."

"Me too. Dad's going to try the motor. There's something a little wrong with it, but if he can get it going, we'll go out. You'll see how much fun it is really sailing."

Rachel looked around. She hadn't even noticed that they were still on land. But it didn't matter. It was enough to look over the water. It was just like sailing. It wasn't even necessary to go out to sea and worry about Life Preservers.

Gladys showed her the little kitchen. She called it the galley; it had neat shelves with little railings for white and blue dishes and there were shining copper pans and pots arranged in places according to size.

Gladys's mother spread a cloth on a table. She and Gladys put out plates and the wrapped sandwiches they had brought, and Rachel's, too. Mrs. Mahoney made coffee on the little stove.

"Guess it'll have to be some other time," Gladys's father said, joining them. "Looks like this is going to be just one more painting day."

Below and outside they heard a high-pitched, quick barking.

"Here, Muffin!" Gladys called. "He's the one that lives on the dock," she told Rachel. "He belongs to the boathouse. Wait till you see Muffin."

He came bounding up.

Everything was here that anyone would ever want, it seemed to Rachel—even a dog. He came straight to her, wagging his tail and sitting up on two legs. He was brown and ragged-looking and had an ear that flopped down and large round brown eyes. He rolled over and sat up and pulled gently at the girls' skirts, and ran up and down the boat and sat up on two legs again, begging for Rachel's sandwiches. She was glad Momma had put so many in the box. Muffin loved sandwiches.

"Tell about Muffin," Gladys said to her father. "Tell Rachel about Muffin."

"Muffin's a hero," Mr. Mahoney said. "A four-legged hero. Gladys is talking about the time we went out on a three-alarm. This was the middle of the night, twelve-thirty sharp. And this tenement on the lower East Side was crowded with sleeping people. It was stubborn, but we'd about cleared

out everybody when I heard this little dog yapping at my heels, more or less pushing me, you might say, toward the back yard. *Never disregard a warning from anyone* is my motto. A couple of us made our way through to a little lean-to. That's all it was, a little back-yard lean-to, and this little dog running like mad and barking louder than ever. We chopped in the one window and the smoke poured out. We found them just about dead. Mother, father, and youngster. No one had a right to sleep in an old woodshed like that, but there they were. Muffin saved their lives, that's all I can say. It took a little time to revive them, but next day they were all right.

"If you look down there, Rachel, you can see the Hurley house. The Hurleys got the job up here taking care of the boats and the dock, and Muffin came along with them."

Muffin stood up on his two back legs. Mr. Mahoney gave him a large slice of meat out of a sandwich.

Gladys leaned over and whispered to Rachel, "Look at Dad's arm. That's the burn he got that time."

A wide scar extended down from the elbow to the hand.

"And a medal," said Gladys. "A medal for bravery. Show Rachel the medal sometime, Dad."

Mr. Mahoney stood up. "None of that medal stuff," he said.

"You know what a modest man your father is," Mrs. Mahoney said. "We'll have to show Rachel the medal ourselves. He never will."

Gladys told Rachel which was the portside and which the starboard and how to say starboard, and that you say companionway for staircase and galley for kitchen and cruising for a ride on the water.

"See why I stare out of the window on nice days and forget about arithmetic?" Gladys said seriously. "I keep thinking about all this." She waved her hand toward the water side.

"I'm sorry we couldn't take you out on the Sound, Rachel," Gladys's father said, "but that motor isn't in the mood for a ride today. Next time you come with us, we'll go out. I promise you."

"If ever Daddy finishes painting and fixing up

and fiddling with the engine." It sounded fresh, but it wasn't meant to be fresh.

"We're going for a cruise," he said, "way out on the Sound. See if we don't, Rachel. Next time."

Next time. Rachel hoped there would be a "next time." She listened to Mr. Mahoney talk. Even the way he said her name was different, stretching out the *a*, shortening the second half of *Rachel*. Altogether different from Poppa, saying her name the familiar way.

It was not yet dark when they started for home, riding in the trolley again, and looking out over the vast, dusky expanses of farmland and open fields and distant, disappearing water.

Rachel's eyes, shut to overcome the swaying of the trolley, could remember the look of the shining water in sunlight, and the blue sky. She tried to remember the smells of the day, too, and her hand could still remember the rough, round head of Muffin.

Her face felt hot, but it was pleasant, and not as if she were sick and had a fever.

At home Herman said, "You look funny. Did you fall overboard?"

"Fall overboard? I did not! We didn't even go on the water."

Herman was disappointed. "What did you do?"

She couldn't say. They hadn't really done anything to tell about, and yet it had been a crowded day. "We sat on the deck and we looked out over the water. They're painting the boat and fixing the engine."

"Did you paint, too?"

"Everyone has to help on a boat."

She wished Herman could have been along. Really wished it. Because then he would be able to talk about it now with her. Instead she had to think about it all by herself.

"There was a dog, too," she said. "The dog's name is Muffin."

Later she would tell Herman about Muffin's saving people's lives and Mr. Mahoney's medal for bravery.

She helped Herman with Long Division, but through the Long Division she kept seeing the color of the water and the shining white of the boat and Mrs. Mahoney taking out the neatly wrapped sandwiches and opening a Thermos. She had never seen one before. Mrs. Mahoney poured hot chocolate out of it for Gladys and herself, really hot and steaming exactly as if there were a little stove inside the bottle.

"There's a kitchen," she told Herman, "and an icebox and there are real chairs."

"All that in a little boat?"

"It isn't little. It's as big as this room. Maybe bigger."

She looked at herself in the sideboard mirror and was startled. It was sunburn and it was beautiful. She had never been sunburned before. She had bright red cheeks, and the tip of her nose was bright red too. And when she pushed her bangs away, her forehead was white over the line of sunburn.

11

It was Friday evening. The table was set, the brass candlesticks were catching a thousand reflections, and the quince jam was in the very center of the table, transferred out of its jar and ladled into a low glass bowl.

They were all waiting for Boris.

Momma glanced at the clock frequently. "Any minute now," said Momma, "Boris will arrive. You will see. Something tells me he will come tonight. This time we must find out about our old neighbors and friends. I have a thousand questions to ask Boris."

"Boris was so happy to be playing and singing," said Poppa, "we hardly made his acquaintance before he disappeared."

"He hasn't disappeared. He has simply been occupied in the theatre. Tonight he will tell us everything." Momma was rearranging the table setting. She told Herman to brush his hair better. Then she said, "Lend me your glasses, Lessing. I'll try to read."

It was no use. Momma was too restless. "The more I think of it," she said, "the more it seems to me that the name Rose suits her. What do you think of Riva's new name?"

"Very nice," said Poppa. "Why should she keep an old-fashioned name if a new one has occurred to her?"

"Yes," said Momma, "Rose is far from old-fashioned. Did you notice she is not afraid of anyone, not even of a policeman? Especially now that she has begun to speak entirely in English."

"She will learn," said Poppa. "In America

we say *Where there's a will, there's a way.*"

"What can be keeping Boris? I am very anxious to tell him our plans for Sunday." Momma looked out of the window.

"He is probably still occupied in the theatre," Poppa said. "Perhaps we'd better not wait with supper any longer."

It was becoming a usual thing. Momma said, "Something tells me Boris will come tonight," and everyone expected him. Tonight, as on all the previous evenings, Boris didn't come. Nor did he come the next evening. Nor the next.

When Momma asked Poppa for Boris's address in order to write him a letter, it turned out that Poppa thought Boris had left his address with Momma. In any case, he hadn't left it. He had simply promised to come again.

"Of course, he is very busy," said Poppa. "You heard how occupied he is with the lights and the settings and the rehearsals. Once that is all arranged, he will come to us. Don't forget that his accordion is still here, aside from everything else."

At school Miss Bannerman praised Gladys. "You did good work, Gladys, on the arithmetic test. You are showing the results of your extra work with Rachel." Miss Bannerman then went on, "But I was surprised to see that *you* didn't do better, Rachel. I had to mark your paper 85."

Rachel didn't mind. She could have told Miss Bannerman why she hadn't done better than 85. It was because she had begun to look out of the window more and more whenever the November skies were clear and the sun shone. Her thoughts traveled away from Ratio to remembering how the water sounded, clip-clopping against the side of the boats. She had been dreaming of it during the test, and all at once Miss Bannerman was saying, "Pens down!" She hadn't even finished answering all the questions.

"I hope you'll do better on the Finals in January, Rachel."

Of course she would. In January it would be too cold to dream about the boats on the water.

Gladys leaned forward and rubbed her two forefingers together. It meant, "Shame!" Then she sent Rachel a note: *You get scolded for 85 and I get praised for 75. There's no Justis.*

Miss Bannerman frowned at Gladys, and Gladys pretended to be busy arranging pencils on her desk.

Miss Bannerman said, after a long pause, "My class has always presented the Final Assembly Program. I think we have some candidates here. Harold Rosen, will you play a violin solo?"

Harold looked doubtful.

"I think you can," said Miss Bannerman, answering for him.

"Yes, ma'am," said Harold, still doubtful.

"And Rachel Lessing, I'd like you to learn a long poem."

She loved to recite. Miss Beck used to say that she read with more expression than anyone else. Miss Bannerman must have noticed, too, that she read with expression.

"Yes, Miss Bannerman," Rachel said.

"Rachel and Harold, stay for a while at three o'clock. We'll have to rehearse, you know. We can arrange the time for rehearsals this afternoon."

It reminded her of Boris. Now she, too, was going to have rehearsals. She glanced over at Harold Rosen. Harold was one of the good boys. He sat in the back of the room. Miss Bannerman never found fault with Harold. He brought his violin Wednesdays and Fridays. On Wednesdays he went to his violin teacher to take a lesson after school. Fridays he played in the orchestra for the assembly.

At three Miss Bannerman said to Harold, "You bring your violin on Fridays, Harold, don't you? Perhaps we can use the rest of that afternoon for rehearsing. Is Friday afternoon all right with you, too, Rachel?"

It was the day she helped Momma and then, afterward, went to the Library with Lizzie. She looked forward to it all week. She loved to go to the Library, and then Lizzie and she walked each other back and forth between their houses until it was almost dark. But perhaps she could ask Lizzie to go to the Library on some other afternoon.

"I can come any afternoon," said Rachel. "What shall I memorize?"

"'The Blue and the Gray'," Miss Bannerman said. "It happens to be a favorite of mine."

It was in *Stepping Stones to Literature, Book 6,* and it was sad.

"Look over all your pieces, Harold," said Miss Bannerman, "and find something you can really play well. Something that's not too long."

"I can play 'Souvenir'," said Harold. "I play it about the best."

"Very well," said Miss Bannerman. "It happens to be a great favorite of mine."

If Harold could make his own choice, Rachel thought she might try something else, too. "The Blue and the Gray," she told Miss Bannerman, was sad.

"I already read it, and it's sad."

"Would you prefer 'O Captain! My Captain!'?"

Rachel knew that too, and it was even sadder, she thought, than "The Blue and the Gray."

"Yes," Miss Bannerman said, "perhaps 'O Captain! My Captain!' We haven't had that for several terms."

Miss Bannerman said they would need plenty

of practice. "Please be prepared to give me several Friday afternoons. We can't use the auditorium Friday afternoons because of the Glee Club, so perhaps you'd better both come to my house." Miss Bannerman gave them the address.

It had taken only a little while to learn "O Captain! My Captain!" Poppa thought she said it very well.

"When Boris comes," said Momma, "you will say it for him too." Momma added, "Surely he will come next Friday. Something tells me that next Friday Boris will come."

After school on Friday Rachel looked around for Harold. He had vanished. Rachel walked the six blocks to Miss Bannerman's house.

She had never visited a teacher before. Even Miss Beck had never invited her to come to her house. Rachel looked up at the narrow three-story house on 141st Street and at last pulled the door knocker. Far inside there was a faint, echoing sound.

After a long time Miss Bannerman appeared. She looked exactly the same as in the classroom, although Rachel had expected some change in her now that she was at home.

Miss Bannerman led the way. "We'll go to the upstairs parlor to wait for Harold."

She followed Miss Bannerman up the carpeted stairs. Neither had she ever visited anyone who lived up and down stairs in a whole house. The blinds were drawn down in the parlor, and as these were green the parlor was almost in complete darkness. Miss Bannerman lighted the chandelier that cast its dim light only over the center of the room. All the furniture in the parlor was covered with striped tan linen. This room and the hall smelled strongly of camphor.

There was a piano under a brown rubberized piano cover at one wall. Instead of a three-piece set of furniture like theirs, there were five or six large pieces of furniture under their striped covers. Rachel studied the flowered rug and the lace curtains that reached to the floor.

"While waiting for Harold, I'll go over the accompaniment for you, Rachel. Read the poem, please, and I'll go over the piano accompaniment."

Miss Bannerman parted the brown piano cover at the center and threw each side of it on top of the piano. As if the poem were a song that she, Rachel, would sing, Miss Bannerman, she saw, was going to supply music for it.

"I know it by heart," she said. "I can say it aloud."

"Go ahead, Rachel."

Rachel recited:

O Captain! My Captain! our fearful trip is done,
The ship has weather'd every rack, the prize we
sought is won,
The port is near, the bells I hear, the people all
exulting,
While follow eyes the steady keel, the vessel grim
and daring;
But O heart! heart! heart!
O the bleeding drops of red,
Where on the deck my Captain lies,
Fallen cold and dead.

Miss Bannerman played softly at first. She played music that sounded like the sea and like a "fearful trip" in the beginning, and when Rachel said "Fallen cold and dead," Miss Bannerman struck a chord sharply and lifted both hands away from the piano.

Miss Bannerman turned around on the revolving piano stool. "When you say 'the bells I hear,' Rachel, put your hand to your ear, and when you say, 'Where on the deck my Captain lies,' point to the floor and look down. Now once more."

As if from some distant place miles away, there was the faint sound of a bell.

Miss Bannerman went downstairs and, a minute later, Harold Rosen came in. He looked a little scared, and glanced at Rachel and was somewhat reassured. Then he combed his hair with his fingers and straightened his necktie. He took out his violin from its case and tightened the strings. He put it under his chin and tightened the strings again, and then rubbed his bow with rosin.

"Do you require an accompaniment?" said Miss Bannerman.

Harold shook his head. "Just the A, please," he said.

Rachel was impressed with Harold. He sounded like a real musician.

143

Harold hoisted the violin into position at last, and began.

It was so beautiful Rachel shut her eyes. Then she opened her eyes and watched Harold. It was the most beautiful music she had ever heard, even including Boris's sad songs on the accordion.

It was astonishing. Here was Harold Rosen whom she knew from 6A1, with his hair falling over his eye and his tie crooked and his face perspiring, playing music that was making her cry. She only kept herself from crying by blinking hard.

She remembered the name of it. "Souvenir," he had said. It made her think of the sunlight on the water and Gladys Mahoney's boat, and of going away from the water when she had to go home. It made her think of the walk with Herman in the early morning each day through St. Mary's Park, with the squirrels playing under the trees, and of looking out of the window during Arithmetic and seeing the white clouds in the blue sky. All that was in the piece Harold Rosen was playing. Harold Rosen must be the most wonderful violinist in the world, Rachel was thinking, and the piece he is playing is the most beautiful piece of music in the world.

"A little faster," said Miss Bannerman. "You are dragging it out, Harold."

It hurt Rachel to hear even the least bit of criticism of the wonderful music and of Harold.

"Shall I try it again from the last page?" Harold said, pointing his bow at Miss Bannerman.

"That's what we're here for," said Miss Bannerman. "Try it all over again."

He played it again. It was just as beautiful as before. Rachel did not even notice if it was fast or slow.

"Now, Rachel, it's your turn."

The music had driven "O Captain! My Captain!" out of her head. She forced herself to concentrate on "O Captain! My Captain!" Miss Bannerman added a little more piano music as Rachel recited, and then at the end played quickly up and down on the piano to show it was the end.

"More gestures," said Miss Bannerman.

Harold played "Souvenir" through once more, a bit faster. Rachel could tell, since she now knew the piece better.

Miss Bannerman said, "Much improved. We'll have to have rehearsals quite a few times to make all this absolutely perfect. We appear in public only when we are absolutely perfect."

"Yes, ma'am," said Harold.

Miss Bannerman led the way for them to the door downstairs. "Thank you, Rachel. Thank you, Harold."

"Thank you, Miss Bannerman," said Harold, "for helping us."

Rachel glanced at Harold Rosen. It hadn't even occurred to her to say *thank you* to Miss Bannerman. Harold was polite as well as musical.

She tried to think of a way to tell him how beautiful his playing was, but couldn't. Instead, after they had walked without saying anything for a half block, Harold said, "How did you like my fiddle playing?"

"I liked it very much," she said, glad he had asked her so she could at least tell him this, but still unable to find words to express her feelings about "Souvenir" and his wonderful playing. Then she said, "You are musically talented." Boris had once said that to Herman.

"You ought to tell that to my violin teacher. Anyway, I like to play. If I could just play anything I want, I'd play more."

"My mother has a hard time making my brother practice the piano."

"I hate practicing. I know one thing: I'll never be a fiddler."

She could hardly believe it. "No? Why? What *are* you going to be?"

"A lawyer. What are you going to be?"

"I'd love to be a teacher."

"I thought you were going on the stage. With Miss Bannerman. She should play and you should recite." Harold laughed. "Wouldn't that be some act?"

Harold was laughing at Miss Bannerman! And at herself, too. But it was about Miss Bannerman that she minded his laughing. First he had thanked Miss Bannerman for helping them, but now he thought it was funny. Rachel was surprised at herself. She found herself liking Miss Bannerman. And not wanting Harold to laugh at her.

"Good-by," said Harold. "This is my street."

148

She began to hurry home.

It was much better to listen to Harold play than talk. He sounded as young as Herman when he talked, but when he played it was altogether different. His playing made her feel far away from everything. Harold's playing could change Miss Bannerman's parlor into a view of the Sound with boats on it. Harold and his playing were two things.

But when she had come home she couldn't tell if she had fallen in love with Harold Rosen or with his playing. She was in love with something. Maybe it was "Souvenir." She hummed it, remembering how Harold had looked as he played it the second time. She thought he had looked very handsome as he frowned and bent his head.

Looking into the mirror in the sideboard, Rachel said, "Harold Rosen, I love you." It made her feel sad and then it made her laugh.

Herman, coming into the dining room, said, "What's the matter with you, Rachel? Are you talking to yourself?"

12

It was the next Friday afternoon. The downstairs bell rang and Rachel and Herman went out to the hall to look down the stairwell.

"If it's Boris, there is still time to ask him to come on Sunday. We'll all go to Bronx Park with Rose. And Boris must come too."

Lizzie Stein came running up the stairs. "I know it's late, but I didn't come early because I know you go to Miss Bannerman's on Friday. We can still go to the Library though. It's open until six. And it's only five."

"Go," said Momma, "with your friend." Momma looked pleased with Rachel's new friend, Lizzie. Rachel remembered that Gladys had introduced her to her father.

"This is Lizzie," she said. "And this is my mother."

Momma stared at Rachel. "Very nice," she said, more about Rachel's new manners than about meeting Lizzie.

Lizzie stared at Rachel too. And then smiled at Momma.

On the way Lizzie said, "*A Tale of Two Cities* is the best book I ever read. Did you read it, Rachel?"

"Oh, yes. And I loved *Treasure Island*," said Rachel.

"And *The Mill on the Floss*," Lizzie said.

"And *Jane Eyre*."

"Where were you born?" asked Lizzie.

"Downtown."

"I was born in Europe. And all my sisters, too. One of them is twenty."

"Twenty years *old?*"

Lizzie nodded. "I have five sisters, and I'm the youngest. I've never gone to any other school but P.S. 27."

"It's lovely here," said Rachel. She meant it with all her heart, now that she had a Library friend and a friend who had a boat on the Sound, a teacher who thought she could recite better than anyone else and could help another girl with arithmetic, and now that she knew Harold Rosen, who could play "Souvenir."

"I once went Downtown with my mother," Lizzie said. "We went to buy an alarm clock. On a pushcart. They have all sorts of things on pushcarts. They even have toys on pushcarts."

"I know," said Rachel, thinking of the brightly lighted streets and missing them a little, even now. "But this is better. This is my favorite place to live."

At Rachel's suggestion Lizzie took out of the Library *At the Back of the North Wind,* and Rachel took out *Captains Courageous,* because the title reminded her of Miss Bannerman and "O Captain! My Captain!"

Rachel told Lizzie about their bookstore and asked her if she wanted to see it.

"A bookstore? Of course."

They peered into the window. Mr. Winkler and Poppa were talking to each other across the store. They could see Mr. Winkler, standing in back of his showcase of watches and jewelry and watch repairs and gesturing as if he were making a speech.

"That man is Mr. Winkler," Rachel explained. "That one is my father. Next to the books."

"It's like owning a Library," Lizzie said, staring at the shelves of books through the window of the store.

"Come inside," Rachel said.

Mr. Winkler greeted them from his side of the store. "You look like real customers," Mr. Winkler said. "Like big ladies."

She introduced Lizzie to Poppa, and Poppa said, "Here are some books by Horatio Alger and here are wonderful mysteries by H. Rider Haggard and Wilkie Collins. Did you ever read *The Moonstone?*"

"No," said Lizzie.

"You may read them all. Any time," said Poppa.

"Did *you* read them all?" Lizzie asked Rachel.

"All summer in the evenings I sat outside, under the street lamp—there's one right near the door. I finished a book each evening."

Mr. Winkler said to Rachel and Lizzie, "Think how lucky you are. You know how to read at your age and I, old as I am, do not. I, too, would have liked to be in the book business with Mr. Lessing. But as I do not read English, I must be in the watch business."

"I have promised to teach you," said Poppa, "and, as you see, I do not need help to take care of the customers on this side of the store."

"You must be patient," said Mr. Winkler, just as Momma said. "I can tell you, children," Mr. Winkler said to the girls, "as soon as I learn to read and write in English, I will write the story of my life."

"I will help you," said Poppa. "I will bring you a book from Downtown, a beginner's book of English. You will soon be reading and writing English."

Lizzie put her arm through Rachel's on the way home. Once Rachel had thought Lizzie was stuck-up. She could not imagine how she could have thought so.

"I'll call for you Thursday from now on, until the rehearsals are over. We'll have more time then," Lizzie said.

Lizzie was her best friend. They would always be friends. Rachel could not imagine a time when they would not be friends. They walked along the park side of St. Ann's Avenue. The sunset was making the sky deep red over St. Mary's Park. Everything was hushed. Everything was perfect.

Upstairs Momma had prepared supper. Again the house looked as if waiting for Boris. Again the brass candlesticks were set out on the table, the glass bowl of quince jam was centered.

"If Boris doesn't come this evening," said Momma, "you will have to go from theatre to theatre and look for him. Boris said Second Avenue. You must look for him there. Perhaps he is ill and cannot come to us. At least if you find the theatre they may tell you where his hotel is."

"There are many theatres," said Poppa. "And, besides, it may embarrass him to have his family running after him. Let's wait a little longer."

13

Herman was up early on Sunday morning.

"Come on, hurry up, everybody. It's Sunday. We're going to Bronx Park."

Momma had prepared for the trip to Bronx Park as if she were making the journey to America all over again. Everyone carried an extra coat, and Herman carried two big boxes of sandwiches. Poppa was studying a map of the New York City transit system. It was on the inside cover of a memorandum book.

"First we take the trolley on the corner," said Poppa. "That is Step No. 1. Later on, we transfer."

Rose came as they were gathering up boxes and coats. When she heard that Boris hadn't come for several weeks, she shrugged her shoulders. "Well, so, all right. Rachel and I will go for a walk. We'll go Downtown and walk across the new bridge. I haven't walked over it yet."

Rachel thought of the long train ride and how seasick she could get on a long ride. She was very glad to hear Herman say, "Momma said Bronx Park today, Rose. And Poppa too. I want to go to Bronx Park."

"This time come with us, Rose," said Momma. "We'll have a look at the park and walk there instead of across the bridge. It is so cold over water. In Bronx Park there are even wild animals, Lessing says."

"As if we have to go to Bronx Park to see wild animals!" said Rose, laughing. "The streets are full of them."

Herman looked interested in what Rose was saying, but Momma said, "Well, then everyone is

158

agreed. Here are the boxes with our sandwiches. We are ready."

Out of doors it was chilly, with a stiff breeze blowing. The sun was the cool morning sun of approaching winter.

They rode on a trolley and transferred to another trolley, and finally Poppa asked directions of a policeman. In five minutes they had walked to Bronx Park.

It was like leaving the city and coming to the country—fields and woods all about them and towering trees stretching far into the distance. There was even a lake and a boathouse, and brightly painted green rowboats on the lake. Within the last hour the sun had become brighter and the day warmer.

"Like Chernovinsk," Poppa said. "It reminds me of Chernovinsk."

"But more beautiful," said Momma. "It is like Chernovinsk when you have left the town and gone into the country."

Herman at once demanded to see the lions and tigers. Rose, on the contrary, thought she would prefer to see the birds. "The birds," she said, "are something to see, I have heard." Poppa and Momma and Rachel wanted to see everything.

They walked from the elephants to the tigers, from the tigers to the lions. All the animal houses

were crowded with people and all were over-heated and smelled strongly of animals.

Herman darted in and out. He was visible for a moment, then disappeared, and reappeared to beg Poppa to buy peanuts. Poppa let him buy peanuts and Herman fed every peanut to the monkeys. Herman could not tear himself away from the monkeys. "They're like human beings," said Herman. "Sad human beings."

"Let us breathe some fresh air," said Rose. "Come on, Rachel, we'll meet the others later."

Poppa stopped them. "Tell us exactly," he said, "where we are to meet, or we shall each be lost in a different direction."

"The lion house," said Rachel. "Let's meet in the lion house."

"Outside the lion house," said Rose. "Inside —" she held her forefinger and thumb daintily to her little nose. "Anyway, it's better to meet out-side."

The trees were almost bare. The few leaves that clung to them were brown, but the grass was still green. Rose and Rachel walked across the still-green lawns, Rachel aware of a sharp new scent, the scent of autumn.

"This Boris," said Rose, "does he resemble Poppa?"

"A little," said Rachel, "but much younger. He wears a hat made of fur and his overcoat is lined with fur, too. He works in a theatre. He loves to play and dance."

"In a theatre? And where does he dance?"

"He plays his accordion and sings and kicks out his feet."

"I know that dance." Then Rose added, "I like people who enjoy themselves."

Rachel agreed with her. "He loves to play. He left the accordion with us. So he must come back," Rachel said, giving herself this hope too.

They were standing in front of the lion house in the warm autumn sunlight, waiting for the others, when a young man came quickly toward them, a thin, tall young man with a serious, thin face.

"Riva—is it you?" He shook hands with Rose. "I don't even know where you are. You don't believe in postcards? In letters?"

Rose looked coolly at him. Perhaps because he had called her by her old name, or perhaps because of his fine American speech. He had delivered his whole speech rapidly and in English.

"Hello, Jascha," she said delicately. Her face was becoming a lovely shell-pink. "Where I am? I am here. In front of the lions' house."

The young man named Jascha stopped looking serious and smiled at her.

"Do you want to hear some news?" he asked shyly.

"What is the news?" she said, choosing her words and saying them carefully, as if afraid of making a mistake.

"The news is I am now Joseph."

"True? So, anyhow, I am Rose."

For a second he glanced doubtfully at her, wondering if she were laughing at him, then he looked at Rachel. Rachel nodded quickly. Then, seeing Rose looking a little confused, too, and pinker than ever, he began to laugh.

"Well, Rose, how is everything?"

"All right," she said, not venturing further into English.

163

Joseph guessed the reason for her briefness and fell into the soft, easy speech of their homeland. He asked her for her address, and when she gave it to him he wrote it in a little notebook and inquired if he could call for her at eight o'clock. He would like to come then and take her for a walk.

"I am doing very well," he added. "I am working at men's clothing."

"In a factory?"

"Of course in a factory. Have you ever walked across the Delancey Street bridge, Rose?"

"No, not yet."

"Well, then, I shall show you how well built it is and how unshakable it is. It can support us both without bending or breaking."

Rose laughed.

Joseph said good-by, and shook Rachel's hand as well as Rose's.

In a little while Momma, Poppa, and Herman appeared.

"Here you are," said Poppa. "How have you amused yourselves?"

Rachel looked at Rose, who had a surprise

for them. She had met an old friend. Rachel waited for Rose to tell them about Joseph.

She was astonished when Rose said, "We have been waiting for you. That's all." And then she saw that Rose was as shy as Lizzie Stein. She did not want to tell them about Joseph. Perhaps she was afraid they would laugh at her when they discovered she had made an appointment with Joseph in Bronx Park while standing in front of the lion house.

Herman went back to the monkeys after lunch. Momma and Poppa, Rose and Rachel sat on a park bench and watched the rowboats on the lake.

Going home from Bronx Park, Rachel and Rose again walked together, leaving the others a little distance behind.

"What does Boris do in the theatre?" Rose asked. "Is he an actor?"

"No," said Rachel. "He does something else. Rehearsals and lights and settings."

"What is that?"

"I don't know," Rachel said.

Rose said, "It is interesting, this working in a theatre."

Rose left them at the subway on the way home. "I have an appointment this evening," she said. "Good-by, everybody." She bent and kissed Rachel and Herman. "If you see Boris, I send him my best regards." She looked like a little girl as she hurried to the subway.

"We are all disappointed because of Boris," said Poppa. "Even Rose. But he will come. He must come. Haven't we the accordion?"

14

Rachel knew "O Captain! My Captain!" so she could say it almost in a single breath. And she had heard "Souvenir" played by Harold Rosen so many times it no longer made her want to cry.

At last Poppa had decided to go in search of Boris.

"In New York," said Momma, "a person can vanish as if the earth had opened and swallowed him. Ask at each theatre on Second Avenue. Ask whether there is someone who remembers Boris.

Describe him and ask if he has been seen. How many such hats and coats can one find in New York? Someone must surely remember him. There are not so many theatres, either. The best thing would be to go to each one."

Rachel went with Poppa.

There weren't many theatres, just as Momma had said. But most of them were closed this morning. At others, no one at the door remembered having seen Boris, and Rachel and Poppa were not allowed to go inside.

At another a man was putting up an announcement that said:

KING LEAR
A NEW PRODUCTION
By WILLIAM SHAKESPEARE

Poppa said to this man, "Excuse me, I am looking for someone named Boris Lessing. He is a theatrical designer. He arrived in New York not long ago, a tall, handsome young man who wears a fur hat. Did you happen to meet him? I am looking for him—"

"So am I," said the man, continuing to paste up

his announcement and slapping on the paste more violently. "Has he thrown away your money, too?" He turned to Poppa. "Let me tell you about this charlatan. He swears he is the very best designer. World famous. But what does he do? Orders hundreds of yards of fine expensive fabric and then—what do you think? Yes. Asks for more fabric! And more fabric! And when it is refused once, he walks out. Disappears! He is angry! *He* is angry! What name did you say?"

Poppa said quietly, "Lessing."

"It was a different name. Something like Borishevski. No doubt a false name, in any case. You say *you* are looking for him. *I* am looking for him and when *I* find him he will go to jail. And Goldman means what he says!" He stood away from the announcement and fixed his eyes on Poppa.

"Thank you," said Poppa, moving away.

Poppa looked no farther. "We had better go home," he said. "It is getting late."

For some reason Poppa did not tell Momma the story of the man who had been putting up the announcement at the theatre. He said when they arrived home, "I have asked everywhere. He is simply not known."

Then, suddenly, out of the gray, early December sky, just as the first snow flurries fell on the Bronx, who should come in one afternoon, as if he had parted from them only the day before, but Boris.

"Rachel, hurry," said Momma. "Get Poppa. He must be told at once that Boris is alive and well. Rachel, hurry and put an end to Poppa's worries."

Rachel ran to the bookstore. Poppa was on a ladder arranging books on the highest of the shelves.

Mr. Winkler sat beside his counter, his forehead in his hand, his elbow on the counter.

"I was just describing to your father the day of my arrival in America," said Mr. Winkler. "It was a bitterly cold day. I looked at the streets along which the wind blew cuttingly. I saw people walking with their heads buried deep in their collars. In spite of the cold, each had something to do. Each had a place to go to. Only I had nowhere to go. I sat with the other immigrants behind a glass window on East Broadway, wondering if I would ever have somewhere to go and something to do. Suddenly I see my uncle arriving. On his arm is a warm coat—"

Rachel wanted to hear about that first day of Mr. Winkler's in the United States. It was a story very much like those Poppa told. But she had to tell Poppa the news. At once.

"Poppa," said Rachel, "Boris has come back. He is at home."

"Boris is home? What have I been telling you, Winkler? I'll be down at once." Poppa began to come down the ladder, and just as he reached bottom the door was flung open and there were Boris and Momma.

"We came to you rather than have you come home," said Boris, "because I do not want to interrupt you during business hours. I did not want to take you away from your business."

Poppa looked around. Mr. Winkler still sat with his forehead in his hand. No one else was in the store.

"There is nothing to interrupt," said Poppa.

He introduced Boris to Mr. Winkler. Mr.

Winkler removed his hand from his head and shook Boris's hand.

Boris, Rachel noticed, was thinner now. And he had exchanged the fur coat for a thick black and gray checked overcoat, and the fur hat for a large-brimmed black one.

"You look splendid," said Poppa. "Like an opera singer. Like an opera singer from the Metropolitan Opera House."

"I have worked hard," Boris said.

"In the theatre?" Momma asked.

"The world of the theatre," said Boris, "is a harsh world. It demands all and gives nothing. You give it your life. What does it give you? A shrug of the shoulders. Blows instead of praise. No, I am completely through with the theatre. Shortly I will become a wholesaler."

They all stared at Boris. They had no idea what a wholesaler did.

Boris seated himself on the counter on Poppa's side of the store. When he looked up at Rachel and smiled, he looked like the young man who had come to them with the accordion and the valise full of presents, but when he stopped talking, he looked different, as if he were thinking unhappy thoughts.

Momma glanced frequently at him and looked perplexed. "Well, we are glad to see you anyway," she said. "We have been worrying about you and hoping you would at least come to see your relatives, no matter what happened."

Boris raised his shoulders. "I wanted you to see a success. I wanted you to see the results of my work and then—I had nothing to show you. Naturally, I am heartbroken."

"There will be other opportunities," said Poppa.

Boris nodded slowly. "Let us talk to the young ones," he said, and sighed. "They know the secret of the future. Rachel, what are you doing? In school, out of school, tell me you are happy at least."

She had so much to tell him. About the boat and about "O Captain! My Captain!" that she wanted to recite for him. About Peter the Great and about the music that Harold Rosen played. And the only thing she could think of to say was, "One day we expected you. My Aunt Rose and I walked in Bronx Park that day. I said you liked to sing and she said she liked people who enjoyed themselves."

"Who is this Rose?" said Boris. "She sounds like an intelligent person."

"She is my youngest sister," said Momma. "You will meet her."

"For my part, I like intelligent people," Boris said. He looked around the store, first on the side of Poppa's books and then toward Mr. Winkler. "You have only books?" said Boris to Poppa.

"Of course, only books. This is a bookstore. Except for the watches and the jewelry, which are Mr. Winkler's. I should have many more books, of course. In foreign languages, for instance. And dictionaries, too. Many more books, in short."

"It seems to me," said Boris thoughtfully, "it seems to me there are enough books here, and enough watches too. But what does one think of when one has bought a book? Tell me," he said to Poppa.

"Another book, I hope," said Poppa.

"Yes, but there is so much space here. So

much open, unused space, that I have been thinking as I stand and look about—I have been thinking of something with which to fill this space.
For example, one takes a book home to read. It
is raining or snowing and one stays at home and
reads. Do you see what I mean?"

Poppa reflected and Momma nodded. Mr. Winkler looked a little startled.

"No," said Poppa.

"Well, in the rain, one needs—what? An um-
brella, of course. I cannot see how you can do
without umbrellas in this bookstore. And then,
also, one reads on journeys and voyages. In that
case what occurs to you?"

A ship? thought Rachel. Or a railroad train?

"Valises, portfolios," said Boris. "You should
have some of each. I foresee that a few traveling
shawls will also be appropriate and, as you read,
you think of writing. Perhaps writing paper and
equipment such as fountain pens and desk sets."

Momma was looking at Boris intently.

"Tomorrow," said Boris, "I will go and find out
about these things in my capacity as wholesaler.
I will help you to install them. If the business is

too much for you, I myself will be glad to help take care of the customers."

Not a single person had come into the bookstore, all this time, either to look at Poppa's books or to consider Mr. Winkler's watches.

Momma hadn't said a word, but now she said, "But you are describing a department store, Boris. If all these things are brought in, it will be a department store."

"And why not?" asked Boris. "We can have a small department store here. If it grows, it will become a big department store. We can always rent the adjoining store also. What is wrong with that?"

Poppa looked alarmed and Momma said, "Nothing, nothing at all. Boris, you will have to help us. These plans are too big for us alone. As you are able to talk so well and you already know more people than we shall ever know, why should you not manage the store? Arrange it as you like. Bring in those things that you think will be most suitable, and then, you are in business too."

"I have been suggesting exactly this," said

Boris. "I have been making this suggestion to you as I went from idea to idea."

"So far as I am concerned," said Mr. Winkler, "I welcome you. Personally, I welcome you."

"Of course," said Boris, "if something should come up in the theatre that requires my presence there—"

Everyone looked downcast, except Momma. "On days when you must be away, someone else can take your place. Even Rachel can help after school on days that are too busy," said Momma, looking around the bookstore as if she could already see crowds of customers.

Boris smiled his wide, happy smile. It was like the first evening that he had arrived.

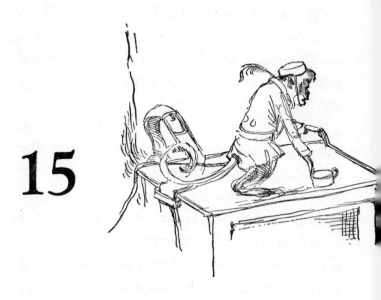

15

The quince jam that had gone back and forth from the table, while they waited for Boris to arrive, tonight stayed on the table.

Momma was beginning to set the table for supper when she said, "Where is Herman? I haven't seen Herman all afternoon. It's getting dark and Herman isn't home. Rachel, ask next door. See if Herman is playing with David."

David was alone. "You ought to see Herman,

Rachel. He was going along with the monkey this afternoon."

"Where, David? What monkey?"

"The organ-grinder monkey. Herman was helping the organ-grinder. Didn't Herman come home yet?" said David. "Maybe he went away with the organ-grinder forever. Maybe he got lost."

Rachel hurried back to Momma. "David saw him this afternoon. He was watching the organ-grinder—the man with the Katrinka."

Momma called it the Katrinka and so did Rachel, first because Momma could never learn to say *organ-grinder,* and also because Rachel herself liked the word Katrinka. It seemed to her it suited the music box and the music better than the word, organ.

Momma looked frightened. "The Katrinka? Where can one find a Katrinka in the middle of the night? Where can Herman be?" While she spoke she was undoing her apron and slipping on her coat.

Poppa was putting on his coat, too. "Stay here, Boris. We must go and see if we can find Herman."

"Don't worry," said Boris. "Herman is not a boy who is easily lost."

Rachel and Momma and Poppa were halfway downstairs when they met Rose coming up.

At any other time Momma would have been overjoyed to see Rose, who had come this time at the very moment when Boris had come. Now Momma only said, "Rose, we are going to look for Herman. Herman is lost."

"Let me come, too. Let me look for him, too," she said.

Momma hesitated a moment. "All right. Perhaps it won't take too long. Heaven alone knows what has happened to him." Momma was ready to burst into tears.

Rachel and Rose hurried ahead. Momma and Poppa stopped people and asked them these curious questions, "Did you see a Katrinka? Have you seen a man with a Katrinka and a monkey and a little boy?"

Everyone understood. And everyone said no.

They went down Brook Avenue, and looked to either side.

Then up St. Ann's Avenue and then across

149th Street. No one had seen Herman or the organ-grinder. It grew late. All the light faded out of the sky. In some of the streets the street lamps were far apart and the sidewalks lay half in darkness. They walked on and on. Once they thought they saw a little crowd. And once they thought they heard Katrinka music. But when they turned the corner, there was only silence.

Blocks away from home, turning a corner, Herman ran into them.

Directly in back of Herman was the organ-grinder, his organ strapped on his back and the little monkey sitting on top of the organ, hurrying after Herman.

"Here, boy, take, boy!" The organ-grinder was shouting and waving his hand at Herman.

When the organ-grinder saw Momma and Poppa, Rachel and Rose, he stopped and turned clumsily around, and hurried off in the opposite direction.

They looked at Herman. Even in the darkened street they could see his face was streaked with dirt.

Momma was terribly angry and at the same time very happy. "Where did you run away to?

Tell me," said Momma, not waiting for an answer. "Why was he chasing you? Tell me, Herman, or I will punish you."

Then Momma suddenly put her arms around Herman. She tightly held him and then said, "Come home, hurry up. Tell me everything at home."

"He wasn't chasing me," Herman said. "He wanted me to take the money. Because I helped him."

"What money? How did you help him? Tell me, Herman, or you will be punished," Poppa said.

"He was standing on our corner and no one was giving him pennies," said Herman.

"Which corner? When?"

"When I went downstairs after school. When I went to buy the salt. I was watching the monkey and the monkey took off his hat and nobody put pennies into the hat. Everybody was standing there and watching the monkey and I put in the nickel."

"The nickel I gave you? For the salt?" Up to

this minute Momma had entirely forgotten about the salt.

Herman nodded.

"Then after I put in the nickel somebody put in a penny and then somebody else, too, because I said it's a talking monkey."

"What do you mean you said it's a talking monkey?" said Poppa.

Suddenly Herman stepped away from them. "I went like this: 'Come on, everybody, give the monkey a penny.' That's when they gave him the two pennies. And more people came, but no more pennies, so I said, 'It's a talking monkey. You want to hear the monkey talk? So give him a penny. Come on, everybody.' And more people gave him a penny. Everybody heard me and a lot of people stopped. They were all waiting to hear the monkey talk, so I began to dance for them."

"You danced?" said Momma. "In the street?"

"The dance Boris showed me. And then I stood on my hands. Jimmy showed me how. I showed him how to do the dance and he showed me how to do a double handstand and somersault and land on my feet. And the man was playing the music fast. Everybody began to give me the pennies, so I took the monkey's hat and I collected all the pennies."

"For pennies?" said Poppa. "You were dancing in the street for pennies?"

"For the man and for the little monkey. I was dancing and there were a lot of pennies and two nickels and somebody put a dime in, too. Maybe he put it in by mistake."

"So why didn't you come home after you made such a big collection?" said Momma, still terribly angry and very happy.

"We went somewhere else. We went to St. Ann's Avenue and we went in the back yards, too. And people threw down money when I danced. First I said if they want to hear the monkey talk they must throw down a penny and then I danced and they threw down the pennies anyway."

"Look at your shirt, Herman."

"It got dirty on account of my dancing in it and doing handstands," said Herman.

"And standing on your head," said Momma.

"We got a lot of money. We went to a million

houses. Then the monkey had to have his supper. He gets a banana for supper. The man said, 'No more dancing,' and that's when he wanted to give me the money. He said, 'Hey, take the money.' He wanted me to take half of it because I helped him. So that's when I began to run home."

They walked two long blocks.

"Promise me one thing," Momma said. "Promise me you will positively never run after the Katrinka again. Promise me this or Rachel will have to take you to school and bring you from school. Just like when you were five years old. Herman, do you promise?"

"Sure," said Herman.

Momma sighed a deep, long sigh. "When we come home," she said, "you will have to sit in the bathtub for an hour. It will take at least an hour before you are clean again, Herman."

16

In the bathtub Herman was singing the songs he had learned from the Katrinka. "O Sole Mio" and "La Paloma" and "The Blue Danube," and he was singing "Killarney" too. And also singing some of the songs that Boris had played. Herman had a good memory for tunes. Although the door was closed, Herman's singing filled the house.

"Can I have my drum, Rachel?" Herman shouted from the bathtub. "Bring me my drum."

"Positively no drum in the bathtub," said

Momma. "First you are the assistant to a Katrinka, then you dance in the streets, and now a drum in the bathtub. You are becoming a big musician, Herman."

"How is the homework?" said Poppa. "I didn't hear you say, 'Bring me the arithmetic to do.'"

Momma had already forgotten how glad she had been to see Herman alive. She said, "Herman, be quiet. We are trying to talk and you are making noise."

Boris had made a list, and held it up for them to see.

"Here are the essentials," he said. "These are all useful things we must bring into our bookstore. We will see which ones are the most needed and then we will buy more of this than of that, and of that more than of this."

It was a long list and Boris read it to them.

Rose sat quietly listening and looking up at Boris now and then. She was leaning her chin in her hand and her elbow on the table, and every now and then Boris would look to her for approval.

"I have heard you are an intelligent young

lady," Boris said. "What do you think of wallets in a bookstore of this sort?"

"All right," Rose said, nodding and not daring to trust her English since Boris spoke it so fluently. "Anyhow," she added, "more variety is better." She looked at Poppa and Poppa could not disguise his pleasant surprise.

"How have you learned so much, Rose?" Poppa asked quietly.

"I go to night school now," Rose said, speaking only English now.

"O-ho," said Poppa, "night school! You will soon speak better than all of us."

Rose lifted her shoulders and opened her hands as if to say, "We can only hope for the best," and then she saw that Boris was looking at her and smiling his wide, friendly smile.

She smiled too, and Boris said, "I have a longing to play some of the songs that I love. The truth is, up to this moment I haven't had the heart for it."

"By all means, play," said Poppa. "But you will have to sing louder than Herman."

"He will listen, too," Boris said.

188

Poppa brought down the accordion.

Boris played and sang, song after song. They laughed over the funny ones and Momma cried over the sad ones. And just as Boris said, Herman listened too.

Every time Rachel glanced at Boris, Boris was looking at Rose. It was as if he were singing only for Rose tonight.

There was a ring of the downstairs bell and soon a knock at the door.

Mr. Winkler, breathless, came in. "Excuse me. I know it is late. And I know I should not disturb a family gathering, but some thoughts come suddenly, like a flash of lightning. Only tonight—this very evening—I remembered that a few days ago I was offered a few small diamond rings and some wedding presents for my store. I refused, but now the thought came to me that if you are expanding, I too should expand. Ever since you came in with this young man, I have been thinking of this and making up my mind: shall I expand or shall I not?"

Boris said, "As for me, I am for expansion. But why *small* diamond rings? Let us have large diamond rings. If we are to expand, let it be a great expansion." Boris opened his arms wide.

"We must begin with small diamonds," said Mr. Winkler, "as I have not been offered large ones. But as we expand, as we continue to grow in size, so will our diamonds."

"Very good," said Boris. "Very understandable."

"Before I leave," said Mr. Winkler, "and to celebrate our—our expansion, I have something here for Rachel." He took a small, tissue-wrapped package out of his pocket. "This is too small for a big girl and too big for a little girl. It is only good for someone like you, Rachel, who is not too small and not too big. It was useless up to now, but now, listen." He held the now-unwrapped watch to Rachel's ear. "And what is the right time, please?"

Poppa took out his great silver watch on its silver chain. "Ten minutes past ten."

"Exactly. No more and no less," said Mr. Winkler. "So, Rachel, this is for you."

The watch had a bracelet made of gold links that snapped around her wrist.

"Wind it slowly and carefully, Rachel," Mr. Winkler said.

190

"Thank you, Mr. Winkler." Rachel *saw* the watch on her wrist and *could hear* it tick, but she did not believe what she saw or heard.

"If I had a daughter, I would have given it to her," said Mr. Winkler, "but can I give this watch to my son? Of course not. So, it's for you."

She hoped she would be allowed to wear it every day. No one else in her whole class had a wrist watch. Even Gladys Mahoney, who had a boat with a cabin, didn't have a wrist watch. It was like a graduation present long before graduation. She examined it carefully. Small and dainty, it had a little flower painted on the white dial, and tiny black numbers. It was too beautiful. Suddenly she thought of something. Next Friday was the Final Assembly.

She would have a new watch to wear when she recited "O Captain! My Captain!" When she'd say *The fateful hour has come* she would raise her hand and look at the watch.

"More gestures," Miss Bannerman had said.

The watch would be perfect.

17

The trees in St. Mary's Park were snow-covered now. Little children carried sleds and coasted down the gentle slopes. In the playground the sparrows came to look for the crumbs Herman brought each day.

Every Saturday Herman walked up and down the streets of the Bronx on long walks to see if he could find the organ-grinder again. Rachel and Lizzie went along sometimes. When they heard distant organ-grinder music they hurried to see if it was their organ-grinder. It never was.

Once they told Poppa they had been looking for the organ-grinder all day, and Poppa said, "Wait for the springtime. This is no time for a monkey to be out of doors. It is even cold for Herman, so how must it be for a small monkey with thin fur?"

But in the meantime and while waiting for the spring, already there was magic in the air.

Herman had wanted to see Boris make something vanish. He had. Boris had made the quiet bookstore of Poppa's vanish. In its place there was a busy store full of people.

The books were still there. There were even more than before. There were foreign language books, too, and encyclopedias and children's books and dictionaries. And Poppa was busier than he had ever been, looking through his books, arranging them and rearranging them. But besides the new books there was much more.

There were crowded shelves in the back, and all of the floor space was taken up: valises and umbrellas, portfolios and wallets, handbags and even a Victrola and two shelves of records in envelopes crowded the store.

Poppa and Boris were both busy.

Mr. Winkler's business had greatly improved too.

WE HAVE WEDDING
AND
ENGAGEMENT RINGS

said a neat sign in the window on Mr. Winkler's side.

Boris studied it and shook his head. "We must change this sign. The engagement rings come first. Mr. Winkler, it is necessary to change this sign."

Mr. Winkler meekly did as he was told. He had painstakingly learned the spelling and arranged the loose letters. Now he began work on it all over again.

It was just as Boris had predicted. They even needed Rachel's help. Momma now came in every afternoon, and every day made a new friend or two among the customers.

One day, after a busy afternoon at the store, when Rachel had been helping, she said to

Momma, "We won't have to move back now, will we?"

"Move back?" said Momma. "Why should we move back? And where should we move back to?"

"Downtown," Rachel said.

"I am glad to be away from the crowds," said Momma. "Do you remember the crowded streets? And the kitchen without Improvements? Why should we move back? When the time comes to move we will move, but not Downtown. No, we will move to the West Side." Momma herself was surprised at what she had said, it seemed to Rachel. But Momma went on, "Yes, the West Side. Why not? You remember the ride on a bus down Riverside Drive?"

Rachel remembered it very well.

"Only yesterday," said Momma, "Mrs. Glazer told me she is looking for an apartment on Riverside Drive. When Mrs. Glazer moves we will go and visit her. At least we can look around in that neighborhood."

Rachel couldn't begin to think of the West Side. She loved their house and she loved St. Mary's Park. Most of the girls in her class were her

195

friends, especially Gladys Mahoney and Lizzie Stein. And the new Library had all the books she would ever want. Bronx Park was only a trolley ride away. Harold Rosen had said the other day, "I'm going to Morris High School when I graduate. Where are you going, Rachel?"

"Morris High School, I think," she had said, not even knowing where it was.

Then the next Saturday, when she took a walk with Lizzie, they walked to Morris High School. It was enormous and occupied a whole square block. It was like a castle in a fairy tale, with turrets and arched windows. And it was only a long walk from the house Rachel lived in now. No, not the West Side.

"I love the Bronx," Rachel said. "I want to live here forever."

"For a while," said Momma, "we will stay in the Bronx."

One evening Poppa said to Boris, "This evening I would like to read a book. It will be a great pleasure simply to sit in my own house and read a book, especially as I know you are taking good

196

care of the store. I used to have a few hours each day in which to read and to talk to Mr. Winkler, but that time is gone. Of course, it is much better to be busy, but it used to be very pleasant in the old days." Poppa was looking over his shelves while he said this.

"For instance," Poppa went on, "I have never read *King Solomon's Mines*. I like to recommend books I myself have read."

Boris shook his head. "Any other evening," he said, "I would say yes. Tonight I must refuse to let you read. Why? Because it happens I have tickets for you. This pair of tickets will keep you from reading at home tonight. There is a magnificent performance of *King Lear* that you must see. You will go to the theatre and I will take care of the store. And be sure to look at the stage settings. Those are mine. Goldman has now reconsidered his petty economies. He has come to *me* for advice. So I have decided to accept his apologies. On the program you will find the name Borishevski. I will leave you to guess who this is."

"You won't mind," said Momma, "that we are leaving you alone? That you will be working at the store all evening when you yourself could be going to the theatre?"

"I don't mind," said Boris. "But I am not going to be alone. No. It happens that Rose has promised to come here this evening. If there are more customers than I can attend to, she will help me."

Momma looked greatly pleased. "We will be home as soon as possible. You will come, both of you, won't you, after you close the store to have tea with us?"

"Of course," said Boris, "we are always ready for a glass of tea. And next Saturday when you will take care of the store, Rose and I will go to see *King Lear*. And can you guess whom we shall take with us? Rachel and Herman!"

Momma was putting on her new dress. It was long and black and had a white lace collar. Momma looked at herself in the mirror. "It's a little too fancy," Momma said. "I must take off the white lace. This would be becoming for Rose. For me, no."

198

"It's not fancy," Rachel said. "The white collar makes you look a little like a teacher."

Momma laughed. "Really? A teacher?"

Rachel looked at Momma again and saw that Momma didn't look at all like a teacher—not like Miss Bannerman and not like Gladys's mother. Momma looked like herself in spite of the new black dress with the white collar. Momma looked a little worried and a little happy.

"If I knew that Boris won't be too busy. And if I thought that Rose really wants to be in the store instead of—"

Poppa said, "She has already told me she prefers to be in the store talking with Boris than doing anything else."

"And if I knew Herman would go to sleep early and not suddenly run outside," Momma said.

"I'll watch him. I'll see he doesn't go outside," Rachel said.

Momma was only half convinced. "And you yourself, Rachel, should go to sleep early and not read so much. Your eyes—"

"Come," said Poppa, "it is getting late. We

want to be there at the very beginning. When we return we must tell Boris about everything we have seen. From the beginning."

Rachel watched them leave. When she had allowed them enough time to go down the stairs, she went to the window.

Again she felt as she had that day on Gladys's boat, when everything blurred and merged. From here, from this high place overlooking their street and the corner of the park, she saw Momma and Poppa walk away together on their way to the theatre. They were walking along the streets of Uptown as if they had lived Uptown all their lives.

Already she could imagine their evening and what they would say when they returned, about Boris's lights and settings and the play itself. They would be very happy. She understood them: Momma and her saying Positively no and not meaning it and Poppa who wanted to be left to read in peace. She understood everything and everyone, she felt. She even knew another language. She could understand Gladys and her parents, Boris and his singing and playing, and Rose, who wanted to be altogether American in a hurry. And she understood the little world of the boats and the water, and Muffin and fighting fires. She and Gladys had met in Miss Bannerman's class, but they had arrived there from different worlds, just as Poppa always said.

Instead of this window on the top floor it was as if she were someone in a fairy tale who had set out on long travels and had climbed up to a tall tower. She was seeing the whole world now laid out before her. Perhaps she would write it one day, in a book and—

From the next room Herman called, "Rachel, if we had a dollar we could have a poodle. Tony said he could sell me a white poodle puppy for a dollar. Can we get a dollar, Rachel?"

She would write about Downtown and Uptown, and other children would take the book out of the Library.

"Can we, Rachel?"

"No," said Rachel, "we wouldn't be allowed to have a puppy."

Momma would say Positively no, but later, perhaps, Momma would say yes. She, Rachel, longed
to have a puppy.

"Tony says his mother wants to get rid of them.
Could we have one if it's free?"

"You have to ask Momma," Rachel said. "Ask
Momma tomorrow."

Santa Clara County
LIBRARY

Renewals:

(800) 471-0991
www.santaclaracountylib.org